T0021317

The Belting Inheritance

The Belting Inheritance

With an Introduction
by Martin Edwards

Julian Symons

Poisoned Pen Press

Originally published in 1965 by Collins, London
©2018 The Estate of Julian Symons

Introduction Copyright © 2018 by Martin Edwards
Published by Poisoned Pen Press in association with
the British Library

First U.S. Edition 2018

10 9 8 7 6 5 4 3 2 1

Library of Congress Control Number: 2018955750

ISBN: 9781464210877   Trade Paperback
ISBN: 9781464210884   Ebook

Poisoned Pen Press
4014 N. Goldwater Blvd., #201
Scottsdale, AZ 85251
www.poisonedpenpress.com
info@poisonedpenpress.com

Printed in the United States of America

For Gordon Bromley

Introduction

The Belting Inheritance is a relatively little-known novel written by one of the leading British crime authors of the second half of the twentieth century. Julian Symons' story, first published in 1965, is told with his characteristic concision and wit. Especially intriguing is the way he blends elements of the traditional detective puzzle with a portrayal of life in Britain at the dawn of the Permissive Society. Another appealing and unexpected aspect of the novel is that both the mystery and the social mores of the time are seen from the perspective of an intelligent (if sometimes naive) narrator who is only eighteen years old.

The book begins in a pleasantly traditional fashion as Christopher Barrington explains how, following the deaths of his parents, he came to live at the great house of Belting, domain of Lady Wainwright. Her ladyship had lost two of her sons, Hugh and David, during the Second World War, although two other sons, Miles and Stephen, still live at Belting. Then a letter arrives which changes everything. David, it seems is alive, and plans to return home after years spent in captivity.

Lady Wainwright is overjoyed, but Miles and Stephen are deeply sceptical. They believe the letter has been sent by an imposter, bent on securing part of the Belting inheritance for himself. An attempt to buy him off fails, and David Wainwright – or is he someone else, calling himself by that name? – arrives at the great house. Lady Wainwright is convinced that he is indeed her missing son, but Miles and Stephen are determined to prove otherwise. Soon, a murder is committed at Belting…

Julian Symons was inspired to write this novel after reading Douglas Woodruff's magisterial book *The Tichborne Claimant: a Victorian Mystery*, published in 1957. Woodruff examined the famous Tichborne case, a long-running and highly controversial saga which fascinated the Victorian public in the 1860s and 1870s. Most commentators – including Symons' friend and fellow crime novelist, Michael Gilbert, whose *The Claimant* surveys the case – have concluded that the Claimant was an imposter, but Woodruff was not so sure, stating: "The great doubt still hangs suspended." Symons discussed Woodruff's analysis, and found it preferable to Gilbert's, in his essay on the subject, "The Man Who Lost Himself", which is included in his book *Critical Occasions*. (I wonder, incidentally, if a reconsideration of the essay while writing *The Belting Inheritance* prompted Symons to write the three "The Man Who…" novels which came shortly after this one?)

Symons isn't the only novelist to have adapted elements of the Tichborne story for fictional purposes. Examples include *The Link* (1969) by Robin Maugham, son of Somerset, and more famously Josephine Tey's *Brat Farrar* (1949). Tey's book, and the Tichborne case, are discussed in Mary Stewart's novel of impersonation, *The Ivy Tree* (1961).

So Symons was, to an extent, following in the footsteps of others, but he was not content with that. As he said in notes to his posthumously-published bibliography: "The book is an attempt to put the claimant story into a modern setting, or at least that was in my mind at the beginning. In any event, I… strayed off to other things…"

Indeed he did. What begins as a country-house mystery with a faintly old-fashioned feel about it turns into something much more in keeping with the ethos of the 1960s, as Symons charts young Christopher's sexual awakening, and even takes him off to bohemian society in Paris; there is also a sequence of unexpected plot developments. Symons is widely perceived as a scourge of traditional detective fiction, on account of his trenchant criticisms of many vintage mystery writers, but in fact he wrote a good many short stories in the classic vein, while his most effective novels combine insights into character and social attitudes with plotting so clever that Golden Age novelists would have approved. One of the reasons why *The Belting Inheritance* is such an intriguing book, quite apart from its intrinsic merits, is this combination of two types of crime story, the classic and the modern, this blending of literary references and clues with a storyline full of sexual tensions.

Symons was noted for the severity of some of his critical judgments; these did not always endear him to his fellow crime writers, but in his defence it should be said that he was an especially harsh critic of his own fiction. For many years he regarded this novel as a failure, because of the part played in the storyline by coincidence, but in later life he came to take a more balanced – and, I would say, more accurate – view.

In the course of his long life (1912–1994), Symons published poetry, biography, history, works of criticism, books about real life crimes, and even a little volume called *Crime and Detection Quiz*, as well as fiction. Although he became dissatisfied with his early detective stories, he proceeded to establish a reputation as one of the world's leading crime writers, admired by the likes of Patricia Highsmith and Ruth Rendell, with whose fiction his finest novels bear comparison. The range and variety of those novels is impressive: *The Man Who Killed Himself* is a brilliant and often very funny study of a man who creates a second and more exciting identity for himself, while *The Blackheath Poisonings* is a highly accomplished Victorian mystery, and *The Players and the Game* a superb story distantly inspired by the Moors Murders.

In an essay for *Contemporary Authors* (1986), Symons wrote: "Somebody said recently that I am perhaps the most honoured of modern crime writers. It rarely feels like that… but I have valued particularly the Presidency of the Detection Club, in which I succeeded Agatha Christie, and the Grand Master Award from the Mystery Writers of America in 1982". *The Belting Inheritance* is an entertaining example of a Grand Master at work.

Martin Edwards
www.martinedwardsbooks.com

Chapter One
How I Came to Belting

It was a hot day in late July when I sat with Uncle Miles at Belting beside the strippling ream. The deliberate Spoonerism was Uncle Miles', and it did seem to express something about the stream that rippled beside us as we sat on the spongy grass. To say strippled rather than rippled conveyed something subtle about the movement of the water, and ream instead of stream suggested that large bream waited in it ready to be caught. At least, that was what I thought at the time, although I had never caught anything in it that was more than twelve inches long.

The strippling ream or the rippling stream was, in any case, a pleasant place to sit. Uncle Miles had on the back of his head the panama hat which he always wore on a warm day. He stared across the stream at the small field we called the paddock, I lay on my back and stared up at the blue but cloud-flecked sky.

"This is a pretty kettle of horsefeathers," Uncle Miles said in his jerky, rather nervous way, and went on. "Don't suppose you've ever seen the Marx Brothers. Too young."

"One film, *At the Circus*. Not very good."

"They were real comics, wonderful clowns. *At the Circus* wasn't quite vintage, mind. I saw *Animal Crackers* nine times in seven weeks."

One of the clouds was in the shape of an island. You sailed through the sky and landed in the small bay on the southern side. And then what happened? "Why is it a kettle of horsefeathers?"

"Because because," Uncle Miles said. His voice seemed to come from far away.

"Won't you be pleased if Uncle David's alive? Didn't you – don't you like him?"

"It's not a question of that," Uncle Miles said rather pettishly, although he did not say what it was a question of. I took a book from the jacket that lay beside me. "What are you reading?"

I held up *Works* by Max Beerbohm, and quoted from memory the last of those seven essays, "Diminuendo": "Once I wrote a little for a yellow quarterly. But the stress of creation soon overwhelmed me. I shall write no more. Already I feel myself to be a trifle outmoded. I belong to the Beardsley period." As soon as I had spoken the words I regretted them, for I feared that Uncle Miles would take their application personally. I ended rather lamely, "Wonderful to publish your collected works at the age of twenty-four," and then rolled over on my stomach to look at him. I could not see the expression on his face, but the corners of his mouth were turned down in disapproval.

All of this happened long ago, and it seems to me much longer, and I see it as if I were looking through the wrong end of a telescope at figures quite lifelike but extremely minute. Yet that is not right, for a telescope does not distort, and what I want to convey is that my vision and understanding of the things that happened, at Belting and elsewhere, during that summer was a distorted one. It was distorted by my ignorance of the past, for I have noticed that the past only becomes real to us as we grow older, but more still by my own age, or rather youth. I was eighteen, I had that very term left school and was waiting to go to university, and anybody over twenty-five seemed to me old. Nowadays I am inclined to think that middle-age does not begin until forty, or perhaps even forty-five, and it is a consequence of this that the people in the story seemed to me much older than they were, or at least than I should feel they are today. Uncle Miles, for instance, was in his late thirties, although at the time I should have felt him and a man of sixty to be very much of an age. Even Uncle Stephen, stiff-collared, stiff-necked and incredibly rigid Uncle Stephen, was only a year older than Uncle Miles.

I have begun with Uncle Miles and myself beside the stream, and that is as good a place to begin as any, but I ought to cast back a little, to say something about myself and about Belting, and how I came to be there. First of all, Belting. I have not been to Belting for years and shall never go there again, and I cannot trust my memory to give the picture that you, as reader, would see if you went to Belting today. I went there to live when I was twelve years old, and in my memory it is an immense house, one where I used at first often to lose myself. I can remember going up the big staircase and standing on the galleried landing at the point where the south and west wings met, and wondering which of three corridors to take. Each of them looked at night, and even in the daytime, dark and uninviting, and two of them, still more sinisterly, turned sharply after a few feet so that to go down them was to face a double unknown threat.

It might be thought that the natural thing was to go down the third corridor, but the dim bluish electric light half-way down it seemed to reveal at the other end the shadow of a humpbacked man – the Deadly Humpback I called him to myself – poised waiting for me. It was not much of a light and hence it was not much of a shadow, but it was enough to make me wary of going down that corridor. I never did discover exactly what caused the shadow, but the width of the corridors varied at certain points, and these wider places were often filled with bits of old military junk, trunks, and all sorts of relics of the First World War. There was in one corridor a collection of German caps and helmets from such units as the Uhlans and the Death's Head Hussars. I remember that I used often to try on the Death's Head helmet. It must have belonged to a hussar with a very small head, for it seemed to fit me quite well. Some such collocation of relics was no doubt responsible for the Deadly Humpback and in a way of course I knew this, but I was frightened just the same.

It was a frightening house, at least to a nervous boy of twelve who was received there only because of the death of his parents. My father, James Barrington, was a film director. He had married my mother, Sarah Wainwright, very much against the wishes of her family. Her father Jonathan would, I think, have forgiven their runaway marriage, but her aunt Lady Wainwright would have none of it. She had met my father once, and strongly disapproved of him. He was a film director, he drank heavily, and he professed a rather noisy republicanism. It would hardly have been possible to find a combination of qualities more detestable to Lady Wainwright, who (as I learned later) regarded the cinema as one of the most corrupting influences in modern life, had a horror of drunkenness, and thought the Royal family our most valuable bulwark against the insidious advance of Socialism. I have never discovered what my father said or did on his one visit to Belting, but it must have been something that was to Lady Wainwright irrevocably awful. In the many references to my mother's family that I heard my father make, "that old bitch Lady W," figured always as an ultimate obstacle to reconciliation, certain not only to repel any advances but to do so in the most painful way. I think, even so, that my father would have been inclined to risk making an advance, not to Lady W in person but to Jonathan. It was my mother who would have none of it. She was fiercely independent, and when the family cut off contact with her after her marriage, she was prepared to be as unrelenting as they. She must, as I think of it now, have been herself an unforgiving woman, a kindred spirit to her aunt. At the time I knew only that cards arrived at Christmas from her father and from somebody who signed herself "Your Aunt Jessica," but that their names were never on the list that was carefully prepared in our home.

I have said that my father was a film director, and that is what he called himself, but I doubt if he ever really directed any films. He must have been, it seems to me now, one of the hundreds of people who hang about on the fringes of the popular arts, employed in vague occupations with high-sounding names. I remember that once or twice when my mother took me to the cinema she would nudge me and say that there was my father's name on the screen. I was a slow reader and saw the name, but did not quite take in the function to which it was attached. Certainly it was not displayed as, I now know, the name of the director is, on its own in large type. Certainly, too, we did not live in what might be called a film director's way. Our small modern red brick semi-detached house at Woking had, as my mother said, a lady's pocket handkerchief of garden in front and a man's pocket handkerchief behind. When the war came my father found it more difficult to get work in films. Before long – I am hazy about dates and have not troubled to look it up – he joined the Army because, as I remember him saying, there was nothing else to do. My mother became a teacher, a job for which she had equipped herself by taking a teacher's training course. I went to the local state school. I remember my father coming home, very dashing in uniform. He became an officer, eventually got into some branch of the forces concerned with film making and did rather well.

I never understood much about the war, nor was I much interested in it, and the war years tend to repeat themselves in a pattern in my mind. Father would come home on leave, bringing presents, taking my mother out for what he called "a night on the town," coming back very noisy and even once or twice being brought home. Then he would be gone, and ordinary life would begin again. I accepted the war, shortages, occasional bombs, as ordinary, a natural way of life. At one time Lady W must have suggested that my mother and I should go to live at Belting, for I can remember my mother and father talking about it on one of his leaves. He was all in favour of it, as I suppose he had really always been in favour of reconciliation with her family, in spite of those references to Lady W. But my mother would not hear of it. Our contact remained confined to the Christmas cards.

This was true, even after the war ended and my father came out of the Army. I have said he did well, and he had made friends there (although he did not call them friends but "contacts"), so that he no longer had spells out of work. My mother gave up the teaching job, and there were long discussions about whether we should sell the house in Woking and move nearer the film studios. This had been decided, and we were negotiating to buy a house near Gerrard's Cross when suddenly my whole life was changed. My father flew out to Spain for some location work on a film, and for once took my mother with him. The plane crashed near Granada, and everybody in it was killed. While they were away I had been sent to stay with some neighbours named Parker, the parents of Billy Parker, who was a friend of mine at school. I can remember hearing them say, "How shall we tell him? How can we ever tell him?" While they were brooding on this, I heard about the crash on the radio.

To be orphaned at the age of twelve sounds a terrible thing, and seen objectively it is terrible, but at the time I hardly took it in. Everything happened in such a whirl that I was conscious of excitement more than grief. No doubt this wouldn't have been the case if our family circle had been a close one, but I had seen my father very little since I was four years old, so that my memories of him were rather those one has of a stranger who brings occasional presents than of a father who has emotional contact with his son. My relationship with my mother was much deeper, but she was a woman who thought of tenderness as softness. She looked after me in the most exemplary way, making sure that I went to school neat and tidy, putting me to bed when I had a cold, helping me with homework, but she flinched always from close emotion. This was part of her character as a proud, independent woman. Her mother had died when she was a girl, and I am sure she would have felt it inexcusable softness to forgive her father. When he was ill during the war she never visited him, and although she went to the funeral she told me afterwards that she hardly spoke to any other members of the family. She did not want me to grow up with that kind of softness in me. That would seem to a psychiatrist a superficial way of looking at it, but it is deep enough for me.

Even so, the gap left in my life was enormous, and if I had gone on living in Woking and going to the same school no doubt this would have been borne in on me, but I soon understood that my way of life was to be changed. It seems to me to have been within hours of my learning of my parents' deaths, and certainly it must have been within a day or two, that I was visited by Lady Wainwright. I can remember as well as though it were yesterday being told by Mrs Parker that there were some people to see me, and going in to the Parkers' untidy and rather dirty sitting-room. There sat a formidable-looking old lady dressed in what I remember as dark blue velvet, and wearing a tall hat with a black feather in it. A little baldish red-faced man was also in the room, but I had no eyes for him, but only for the old woman. I knew instinctively that this was the old bitch, Lady W, and before she could tell me so I blurted out her name.

She had taken one of the hard chairs, while Uncle Miles— for he was the little red-faced man – sat in one of Mrs Parker's easy chairs. When I mentioned her name she jerked up her head. Her face was fierce as that of a hook-nosed bird, her voice sharp as though words were some hard substance at which she pecked.

"How did you know who I am? Did your mother show you my photograph?"

"No." I did not know what to say next. I could not tell her how I knew.

She paused, looked at me with that fierce gaze, and said it did not matter. "I was very fond of your mother, did you know that?"

"No," I said again, staring in fascination at her hat.

"She was my niece, you knew that, I suppose. I am your great-aunt." I managed a nod. "But she would have nothing to do with me. That was very stupid."

"Mamma," Uncle Miles said warningly, and I almost burst out laughing, it seemed to me so funny that this little bald man should say "Mamma" in that tone of voice.

"I don't believe in sentiment," Lady Wainwright said, and it might almost have been my mother speaking. "You know that your mother and father are dead, and you are old enough to understand what that means."

"He's an intelligent boy, his school says so." That was Uncle Miles again, and again Lady Wainwright took no notice.

"Your grandfather, my brother-in-law Jonathan, is dead, so it devolves upon me to look after you. At least, I feel it to be my duty. You would live at Belting. Have you heard of Belting? It is my home, and it is a beautiful house. You would be treated as one of my own family." As though suddenly conscious that there was another person in the room, she said: "This is my son, Miles. He is in fact some kind of cousin of yours but you may call him Uncle."

"I know," I said. "From the Christmas cards."

Lady W drew her brows together. Uncle Miles popped up with a jerky movement, shook my hand, said "How do you do, Christopher," whispered loudly in Lady W's ear, "Father's family," and sat down again. She nodded.

"I have been in communication with your father's family, and they would be agreeable to this arrangement." From the little I knew of them I could imagine that they would not welcome the idea of looking after a twelve-year-old boy. "What do you say, Christopher?"

I had wept when I first heard of my parents' deaths, but

this was the first time after hearing the news that I felt like weeping again. I was faced with an act of choice, but I knew even then that in any real sense I had no choice at all. What would become of me if I said no? It was not that I wanted to say no, but that I felt the humiliation of being a thing rather than a person, a thing that was not wanted by "my father's family," but that Lady W was prepared to accept. I looked down at the floor and mumbled something.

"What's that?" Lady W asked fiercely.

I managed not to cry as I said, "All right."

"I like a boy who can make up his mind," she said as she got up. Uncle Miles got up too, and no doubt he understood something of what I felt, for with the eye that was on the blind side of Lady W he gave me the most tremendous wink.

After that things seemed to happen as if I were in a dream. Outside, Mrs Parker had already packed my things, and Uncle Miles had been to our house, collected my games and toys and put them into a suitcase. Within a few minutes the Parkers' front door had closed on me and I was stepping into an enormous old-fashioned Daimler, which had a speaking tube between the chauffeur (who disposed a little contemptuously of my small cases) and the back seats. I can remember perfectly that my feeling as I got into the car was one of regret that Billy Parker was at school, and could not be there to see me drive away.

Chapter Two

The House and the People

What was Belting like? I have thought about the way in which I ought to describe it, without much success. At first I thought that I would extract the description of the house in Pevsner's *Kent*, but Pevsner's interest is naturally enough in it as a Victorian Gothic eccentricity, and the account of spires and flying buttresses doesn't bear any relation to what I saw and felt at the time. And since that is the really important thing, that is the way I have decided to put it down.

The Daimler drove through an entrance each side of which was guarded by a battered but formidable stone lion, down what seemed an endless tree-lined drive, clattered across a cattle grid, and debouched finally into a wide gravelled courtyard. My immediate reaction as I looked at the forbidding spires of the Victorian Gothic front that seemed to stretch endlessly upwards was that I was being taken to live in a church. I went very hesitantly inside, snatching off my school cap, and found myself in a great hall with enormous doors leading off it.

Almost straight ahead there was a winding staircase which led up to a gallery that ran round three sides of the first-floor landing. Bits of armour and out-of-date weapons—assagais, Zulu shields, old muskets, swords—lined the walls. In one corner was what I took to be a sentry box. In fact it housed the telephone, but for a long time I was afraid that somebody would leap out from it and attack me. But the thing I hated most was the prevailing gloom. The house was dark, Lady W was mean in small matters, and at some time in the past she had been told that daylight lamps were better for the eyes than ordinary yellow electric light. The hall and all the corridors, both upstairs and down, were bathed in a funereal blue glow. When I was upstairs, in a bedroom which I had been told would be mine and which was four times the size of my room at Woking, I sat on the bed, looked round the vast spaces and at my toys which had been dumped in the middle of the floor, and began to cry. I was crying when Uncle Miles came in.

"What's up?" He looked round. "It is a bit of a barracks, I agree. But you'll get used to it, you know. Nice to have a bit of space, really. I say, what's this?"

I sniffed. "It's a mechanical bowler."

"Is it, now. How does it work?"

He was down on the carpet examining the bowler, and I joined him. We found the mechanical batsman, the fielders and the wicket, Uncle Miles pushed aside a section of the carpet, and we began to play. His enjoyment of the game, as of all children's games, was prodigious. "Be careful, here comes a devilish googly," he would say, or "Oh, good shot, sir, right through the covers… a classic off drive brilliantly caught, he's a fine field, that man." Crouched on the floor, his bald head shining and his face intent, he played this cricket game with me until there was the sound of a gong. He leapt up.

"Good God, young Christopher, it's dinner. We must go down."

"Can I go down with you?"

"I don't think exactly *with* me, that wouldn't quite do, you see, Mamma wouldn't want you to be under my wing as you might say. But supposing you *follow* me at a short distance, keep me in sight, eh?" He gave me another of his winks.

Emboldened by the wink, I said, "Who'll be there?"

"Mamma, of course. You don't want to let Mamma worry you. She won't eat you, though she may look as if she will." He gave a short bark of laughter. "My brother Stephen. And his wife. That's the lot."

While he had been saying this, Uncle Miles had been splashing water over his face from the washbasin in one corner of the room in a rather ineffectual way. Now he straightened his tie and smoothed down his little fringe of hair.

"You live here, don't you?"

"Yes, I live here." There was nothing unfriendly in the way the words were spoken, but somehow I asked no more.

Perhaps this would be a good place to put in a few words about family relationships. A family tree is always boring, and anyway there's no need for it, but it may be a good thing to set out just who everybody is, because as will be seen in a few pages it is important to the story. Lady Wainwright was the widow of a general who had been knighted for his services during the First World War, and had died in the Second. She had had four children, all boys. The two eldest, Hugh and David, had been killed in the war, so that only Stephen and Miles remained. As to my relationship with them, I have already said that my mother was Lady Wainwright's niece. That is as clear as I can make it, and I hope it is clear enough.

I can remember very well dinner on that first night, not

the things we ate but what seemed to me the enormous room with its dark oak panelling, the pictures staring down from the walls, and Thorne handing round the food. I was uncertain what knives and forks I should use and that bothered me a little, but what really worried me was that a man should be hovering about, as I felt, to make sure that everything on the plate was eaten. I very soon came to know that I was misjudging old Thorne, who was a sort of general factotum playing the parts that in other days would have gone to several servants. Apart from Thorne, there was a succession of daily helps, most of them young, and Lady W's maid Peterson, a starchy lady with a moustache. She was a general female factotum as Thorne was a male one, and the running of Belting devolved largely upon them, for apart from occasional bursts of enthusiasm, Lady W took little interest in household affairs.

We sat down five to table, as Uncle Miles had said we should. I did not take to Stephen or Clarissa, and I saw at once that they did not take to me. I have never seen a man so tight and boxed-in as Uncle Stephen. I called him that, since if I was to call Cousin Miles Uncle, it was only natural to apply the same name to Cousin Stephen. The tightness came partly from the clothes he wore, stiff white collars that seemed always half a size too small for him, ties knotted to strangulation point, and suits that managed to be at the same time baggy and tight, baggy at his thin chest and tight at the hips, where he was big without being at all a fat man. The parting in his hair might have been made by a knife, and beneath it his face was white and intense, sharp nosed and thin lipped. When he spoke it was as though words were butterflies which had escaped from his mouth, and which he was trying with sharp snaps to retrieve. There was something about the passion with which Stephen tore a bread roll into pieces, the savage, loving care with which he dissected a piece of fish, that remains with me still.

Clarissa was a red-faced loud-voiced woman who was somehow, for all the loudness, not in the least jolly. She wore rather tweedy clothes, and was passionately fond both of hunting, and of breeding bull terriers. Perhaps it was in sympathy with the bull terriers that her own legs were bowed. I thought at the time that I had never seen anybody like her before in my life, and this was an accurate observation, for there are no such people in Woking.

Dinner could not in any case have been a comfortable meal for me, but it was made worse by a sense that I was on trial, that Uncle Stephen and his wife were waiting for me to make some mistake that would exclude me from Belting for ever. I subconsciously realised that Lady W and Uncle Miles were on my side, and that Uncle Stephen and his wife were against me. I did not understand, however, that their wishes were of no importance, since what Lady W wanted was what happened at Belting.

After dinner we went into the drawing-room. The whole of Belting seemed to me then so strange that this was no odder than the rest, although I did think that it was extraordinarily cluttered with furniture. It was in fact a remarkable room, for Lady W had preserved it as nearly as possible as a drawing-room of the late eighteen-eighties. It was a kind of museum piece, except that this museum was lived in. There was a dark flock wallpaper, the curtains were of dark red velvet with tassels and a fringe, above the carved mahogany chimneypiece there was an ornamental mirror. Vases and ornaments stood everywhere, in all sorts of niches and on little tables. There were four highly decorative clocks, two glass domes containing wax flowers and fruit, mahogany tables covered with dark fringed cloths and inlaid mahogany cabinets. The fireside and wing chairs were, however, very comfortable, and Lady W had so far succumbed to modernity as to permit electric lighting—and not daylight lamps, either—to replace gas.

Miles and Stephen excused themselves after they had drunk coffee, and Clarissa went off to look at something in the stables, so that I was left alone with Lady W. She told me to come and sit beside her, and I went over and sat on a cushion at her feet.

"Do you think you will like it here, Christopher?" She checked herself abruptly. "That's a stupid question, don't bother to answer. Let me tell you something about Belting. I love it myself, and we can all talk about the things we love."

She told me then that Belting had been the family home of her husband, General Wainwright, and that he had brought her there when they were first married before the First World War, an unimaginably long time ago. She talked about him, and about the great work on the Egyptian Wars that he had been engaged on for years when he died in nineteen-forty.

I interrupted her. "That was Arabi, wasn't it? And he was beaten at Tel-el-Kebir."

My knowledge came only from a history book that we happened to have at home, but she was delighted. She pressed my hands together in her two hot old ones, and said that I should help her with the book—for since her husband's death she had dedicated herself to the task of finishing it. She had said that I might wander round the room and so, while she was telling me the history of the house I did so. I looked at the wax flowers which fascinated me, and at a small stereopticon in which pictures appeared to be three dimensional. Upon the top of a carved mahogany grand piano there were a number of photographs in frames. She told me to bring over one, which showed two young men in uniform. When I brought it to her she sat looking at it with a face like a mask. Above it her white hair, which I had not seen beneath the hat when she first came to see me, was piled up with wonderful care.

"Hugh and David," she said. "My two elder sons. They were both killed in the war."

Looking at the photograph I could see a likeness to her in the beaky noses and in the eyes. I asked what Stephen and Miles had done in the war.

"Stephen was in a *reserved occupation*. And Miles—Miles has never been any use. Do you play the piano?" I shook my head. "Hugh played the piano, that one over there. It hasn't been touched since he died."

"When did he—"

"He was killed soon after D-Day, in France. David was a bomber pilot. He was shot down. Sometimes I think I died with them." She said almost angrily, "Put them away. Put them back where they belong."

Now that I pause to re-read all this the whole thing seems to me immensely Victorian, and I suppose that what existed at Belting was the shadow of a Victorian situation. Lady W's determination to perpetuate the glories of the Wainwrights was always touched by her knowledge that this kind of thing was out of date, just as she knew that there was something ridiculous about preserving the drawing-room as a museum. She knew that it was absurd, but she was serious about it too, and she exerted on Stephen and Miles the power that a strong personality has over weaker ones. Stephen worked in a desultory way as partner in a firm of surveyors in Folkestone a few miles away, and had lived at Belting all his life. When he married it must have seemed to him natural that his wife should make her home there too. Miles had come to live there near the end of the war, in circumstances made known to me later on. In one sense it was true that they couldn't get away from Lady W, but in another way they were simply waiting for her to die.

Her husband had been killed in one of the early German raids on London, and he had died without making a will, so that the house and all the money had come to her. I gathered that there was a great deal of money, although she never said so; or talked about it in detail. But Thorne, of whom I saw a lot in my early days at Belting, once told me that General Wainwright could have bought up the whole surrounding countryside if he'd a mind to, and both Stephen and Miles left me in no doubt that there was a lot of money, and that it would come to them. I gathered that when she died they expected that the house would go to Stephen as the elder, and that the rest of the estate would be divided between them. I once heard Clarissa complaining bitterly to Stephen of all the work she had to do. Why couldn't there be a proper cook, proper housemaids? Such things were obtainable even in these days, and goodness knows there was enough money. Why didn't Stephen say something? Stephen glanced at me and said that little pitchers had long ears.

As far as I know, neither Stephen nor Miles dared to speak to Lady W about the money, or to criticise her in any way. She made little secret of the fact that she despised them both, and that her heart had been given to her two elder sons. The moustached Peterson told me one day of her reaction when she heard of both their deaths, within a matter of weeks of each other.

"She shut herself up for two weeks, and she never ate or drank in all that time. And when she did come out, her hair that was black with just a few streaks of grey in it, had turned pure white."

That turning of the hair white, which looks slightly comic and implausible now that I put it down on paper, impressed me greatly at the time. Stephen and Clarissa had no children, and I think it was partly for this reason that Lady W "adopted" me. I put the word in inverted commas because there was no actual adoption, nor any firm arrangement ever made about my position. If she had got tired of me she could, I suppose, have cast me out, although I am sure she would never have been guilty of that inhumanity. She was a possessive and lonely woman, and in many ways far from an admirable one, but she was never anything but kind to me. I suppose she enjoyed being able to talk to me about Hugh and David, as she did during school holidays, when I helped her with research into the Egyptian Wars. This "research"—the word again deserves inverted commas—was carried out in the Map Room (or as Uncle Miles called it the Pam Moor), a bleak cold room with a north light, which had spread out over the floor a great panorama of the positions at Tel-el-Kebir. There was a large expanse of sand, there were Arabi's encampments, there were all the preparations made for Wolseley's decisive night attack. General Wainwright had managed to buy a big collection of Victorian lead soldiers and guns that were approximately of the right regiments (Arabi's troops, I'm afraid, were of a motley kind, but there were a great many of them), and the whole layout really looked very fine. It was a thing to delight the heart of a boy, and I spent hours with the panorama, imagining possible moves that might have been made by either side. Battle prints of the Crimean War looked down upon me, and so did sketches and photographs of General Wainwright, a mild and even gentle-looking man.

My job in the Pam Moor, which was what I called it to myself and to Uncle Miles, was to help Lady W collate the material gathered by her husband in several large boxes, and added to by her. If only she had somebody to organise the thousands of notes in those boxes and put them into proper card index form, she told me, she would be able to finish the book. When I came to work on them, however, I found that the notes were for the most part no more than casual jottings, and that she had not done any work on them for years. What she really wanted was to pour out her feelings about her two dead sons, and she did so to me in that cold, ghostly room, her face alight with eagerness, her dark eyes burning, and the white hair piled like a pyramid above her head. It was David who had helped his father make the Tel-el-Kebir panorama, and David who had made the great battle map that half covered one wall, a map which General Wainwright had said was the best thing of its kind that he had ever seen. Hugh, I gathered, had been more active, he had set up the shooting range I had found at the back of the stables, and had also made an obstacle course I discovered, a course of which the only remaining relics were bits of old pipe for crawling through and a few broken hurdles. David, it seemed to me, had been the arty one, Hugh the sportsman. When I put this idea to Lady W, however—she sat perched on a sort of dais in the Pam Moor and listened to my questions as I sorted out papers and notes—she received it with a frown.

"They were both artists. We are an artistic family. David was a poet, Hugh was a playwright. Are you interested in books, would you like to write?" I said that I would, although I had no idea about it, because I sensed that this was the proper answer. I asked whether Hugh's plays had been successful, and she said sharply that they had not been performed. "Producers are very difficult. But they were both wonderful boys, they would have made their mark upon the world. It is true, Christopher, never forget it, that those whom the gods love die young. I have only one consolation. They both died like Wainwrights."

She told me to go to her room and fetch a black box from her wardrobe. When I brought it in she took a small gold key from her bag and unlocked the box. She did this in a ceremonious way she had, as though the rite was important, and drew out a letter which she read to me in her sharp, clear voice. It was from Hugh's commanding officer, and said that Sergeant Hugh Wainwright had been involved in one of the engagements round Caen on the 14th June, 1944. The fighting had been severe, he had become separated from his men, and the Colonel had with deepest regret to inform her that Sergeant Wainwright was posted missing, and must be presumed to be dead. The Colonel added that Hugh Wainwright had been a born leader of men, and that he had three times refused a commission. She put down the letter and went on speaking, without obvious emotion.

"Five weeks, five weeks to the day after I had that letter, Christopher, I received another." And she read this second letter to me. It was from a Squadron-Leader, and said that Flight-Lieutenant David Wainwright had not returned from a mission over Germany. His Lancaster plane was known to have been shot down, and it was thought unlikely that there were any survivors. In his own hand the Squadron-Leader had added a postscript, "He was a very fine officer."

"Even after those letters I hoped, though I knew it was stupid. Can you understand that? No, you are too young."

I touched a faded photograph. "What's this?"

"David, with the rest of the crew of his plane. The last picture I have of him."

David, with hands on knees, sat in the middle of a group. All of them were smiling. I read the names Flt.-Sgt. M Billings, Sgt. V J Copp, Flt.-Lieut. D Wainwright, Sgt. R H T Williams, Cpl. J H Crump, Cpl. R Shalson, Flt.-Sgt. P Blakeney. I said, "He looks happy."

"Yes."

"Why don't you have it framed and put with the other photographs?"

"I don't know. Yes, I do. It's the last one. I couldn't bear to have it looking at me."

More out of embarrassment than for any other reason, I said, "What about Uncle Stephen and Uncle Miles?"

"Stephen was doing what was supposed to be war work. In an office. Miles was an actor."

"An actor," I repeated in surprise. That seemed to me a glamorous occupation.

"He spent his time with something called ENSA. It was supposed to provide entertainment."

Lady W's code of judgement in artistic matters was peculiar. The idea of being an artistic creator, a poet, a dramatist or a novelist, met with her approval, but to be an executant, an actor, seemed to her vulgar. Or so she said, although I have thought since that her opinions probably reflected her love for her elder children, her contempt for the younger ones. I used afterwards often to look at the photographs of Hugh and David on the piano, and wonder about them. Hugh was wearing a sports jacket, and he was laughing. It seemed to me that there was something in his expression that conveyed a sort of reckless daring. David was in uniform, and looked serious, even solemn. He was very handsome, but I found it hard to imagine him as Lady W assured me he had been, gay and pleasure-loving.

It must not be supposed that I spent all my time with Lady W, or indeed at Belting. I went to the public school where the boys had received their education. The school was in Dorset, in several acres of grounds, a fact which would have impressed me when I first left Woking, but which I took for granted after my first couple of weeks at Belting. I don't want to describe my schooldays in detail because they have nothing to do with this story, but I suppose I should say that I found no difficulty in adjusting myself to public school life. At first I was surprised that the equipment we used and the desks we sat in were no better than those I had been accustomed to in the state school at Woking. The school was not particularly progressive, to use a current word, but after the first eighteen months I found no pressure exerted to force me into a pattern of conformity. Indeed, six years of this school had turned me into a slightly old-fashioned aesthete. I idolised Oscar Wilde, Beerbohm and Rossetti, and admired Appollinaire, Cocteau and Alfred Jarry. I had read a great deal of poetry but very few novels, I knew a lot about some specialised periods of history and had won a History scholarship to the right college (that is, the family college) at Oxford. I had half a dozen friends at school who joined me in forming a society which we called the Æsthetes' Group, but I need mention only one of them, and even he does not come into the story. His name was Sullivan. Looking back on myself at the age of eighteen, I should say that I was intelligent, romantic, and unusually self-contained in my

approach to life and people. When I left school and came
back to Belting, I did not ask friends to come and stay. I had
done so once, and the friend thought that the Pam Moor and
Lady W were both like something out of *Great Expectations*.
The experiment was not repeated.

When I went back this July, at the end of my schooldays,
one thing was different. I had had a letter from Uncle Miles
during my last week, and he told me that Lady W was dying.
She had cancer of the stomach, and it was likely that she
would live for weeks rather than months. Typically, she had
insisted that I should not be told until my exams were over.
"The old thing's *delighted* about the school," Uncle Miles
had written in his emphatic but erratic hand. "*Nothing* could
have pleased her more."

So coming home to Belting this time was different. When
I went to see Lady W I was shocked by the change in her
appearance, even though Uncle Miles had prepared me for it.
She was in the big four-poster bed that she always occupied,
with her face at first in shadow, but when she turned on the
bedside light I saw her white hair lying on the pillow like
strands of dingy wool. There were other things to shock me,
the way the flesh round her great dark eyes seemed to have
been eaten away, the isolation of the nose that was now like
a bit of carved wood sticking up out of her face, the smell
that pervaded the room, but the thing that touched me
most was the change in her hair. Just for a moment then I
understood, as it is difficult for young people to understand,
the life she had lived these last few years, a life that must
have been devastating in its disappointments for a proud
woman like her. I had always been grateful, although at times
my gratitude had been tempered by a feeling that I was no
more than a surrogate for her lost sons, but at that moment
I think I loved her.

She leaned out of bed and grasped my hand with her own, that was thin as good china.

"Have they told you, Christopher? Has that fool Miles told you?"

I could not think what she was talking about, except her illness. I stammered something.

"You came straight up to see me?"

"Of course."

"Then you don't know. I've heard from him, Christopher." I gaped at her. She said impatiently, "From David."

For a moment I thought that illness had affected her mind. Then she groped behind her pillow and brought out a letter written on thin blue paper, in a thin blue envelope. I looked at the envelope. It was addressed to her, and the postmark was Paris.

"Read it, read it." She closed her eyes.

The letter was a single sheet with writing on both sides. I looked for the signature and found it, "Rikki Tikki" with three crosses for kisses beneath it. The handwriting was thin and straggly, sloping down from left to right on the page. I read the letter.

> *Ma chère maman,*
> Read the signature first, I'm afraid you won't rec-
> ognise the writing on the envelope.
>
> I don't know how to begin telling you why I
> haven't written, but I must try. Everyone else in the
> plane was killed, but I only hurt my leg. I was lucky
> enough to find some Germans who looked after me,
> got me German papers. Then when I tried to get
> away across Germany to France my luck ran out,
> the Russians got hold of me. I had German papers,
> and they sent me to a labour camp at a place called

Novoruba. Don't know how long I was there, seven or eight years, or how I lived through it. I think for a time I went a bit crazy.

Damn it, I didn't mean to write about all this, but I'll finish now. They let me out eventually, dumped me in West Germany. I got a job there, then worked my way to Paris, been there for a year doing all sorts of dirty jobs, wondering why I didn't write to you.

Now I have, Dearest Mamma, I know about Hugh and I thought it might be better if I stayed dead too. Stupid. It's a long time, I'm not what I was, but I'd like to come over, see you again. Can I, will you have me? I'm not rich, but you needn't send fare.

This is the comic name I'm known by.

Best to Stephen and Miles.

Rikki Tikki

I looked at the name on the envelope. It was J Stiver, and the address was the Hôtel les deux Pigeons in Paris. I knew what the signature meant, because Lady W had told me during one of our talks. "Tavvi" had been the nearest David could get to pronouncing his name when he was a small child, and his father, who was a devotee of the *Jungle Book*, had called him Rikki Tikki. I put the letter down and looked at Lady W. Squeezed out of her eyes came two large tears. She used the cliché that was, I suppose, inevitable for the occasion.

"It's like a miracle."

"You've written to him?"

"Of course. I told him to hurry over, that he must

come—come and live here. I haven't had a reply yet, no doubt he has things to settle. Then he will come." She stopped talking, moved her hand aimlessly over the coverlet and said with the faintest of smiles, "There's not much time."

Nonsense, I said, nonsense or ridiculous or something like that. I did not know what to say.

"We shall never finish the history now. But you and David—"

"Of course. But don't think about it"

"I want you to understand one thing. David coming back will make no difference, no difference at all, to you."

She was talking about the provision she had made for me in her will, which she had insisted on telling me in detail a few months earlier. When she died I was to receive £20,000 from the estate, and was to make my home at Belting for as long as I wished. It was a handsome provision for the boy from Woking, although by this time I really thought of myself as somebody who belonged here in Belting, in the world where I had been placed.

I left her room a minute or two later, walked along the corridor and met Peterson on the galleried landing that looked down to the entrance hall below. She was carrying, as she so often was, a bundle of washing or laundry. Peterson had never been positively hostile to me, but had made no secret of her belief that it was not possible to make a silk purse out of a sow's ear. She greeted me now, however, almost as if I were a fellow conspirator.

"You've seen her, she's shown you the letter?" I nodded. "Isn't it a cruel trick?"

"A trick?"

"Of course it's a trick. Who would have the heart to play such a hoax on an old lady, and one in her condition. You saw the letter came from France?" Peterson was a Scot, and in her mind nothing but wickedness was to be found on the other side of the Channel. "He said he'd been there for a year, why couldn't he have come over before, will you tell me that?"

It was something I could not tell her, for I had not even considered it. When I read the letter I had not questioned its authenticity. Peterson went on, her moustache trembling with indignation. "It's a heartless practical joke, and whoever did it needs whipping. Using the name he used to be called."

"How would he know the name?"

But Peterson was not to be deflected from her position into answering such questions. "He'll not come over," she said. "Mr Stephen's written a letter that will keep him in Paris for good."

That seemed to me a comparatively enviable fate. At the same time Peterson seemed aware that she had perhaps said too much to me, for now she clasped me by the arms and spoke urgently, with her face close to mine. Under the dim daylight lamps she looked like one of the witches in Macbeth.

"You'll say nothing of this to my lady." It was an order, not a request, and she was not saying My Lady, but asserting proprietorial rights over Lady W. "He is to send a letter saying it will be impossible for him to come."

"Who is?"

"The joker." And with that Peterson picked up her bundle, nodded to me, and disappeared round a corner, bound for a cupboard or storeroom.

I walked down the staircase, through the big hall and out on to the gravelled courtyard in front of the house. Inside the hall it was dark and cool, outside it was bright, and it was brightness I needed at that moment. Old Thorne was laboriously clipping a hedge—although he had twenty different duties inside the house he was always likely to stray outside and work in the garden on a fine day—and I stopped to talk to him. He said nothing about the letter, so I did not mention it. I walked down a small alley lined by privet on either side, which led to a little gazebo. There I sat contemplating the idea that the letter might be a hoax, and thinking about Lady W, until the sound of a car in the drive announced that Uncle Stephen had come home. I got up then and made my way to the stream. There was an uneasy feeling in my stomach, like that one has before an examination or an important interview, and I associated this with my concern that a trick was being played, in one way or another, on Lady W. I could not realise how completely the letter was to change all our lives.

I heard more of the letter, and what had been done about it, at dinner that night. Uncle Stephen greeted me with his customary cold handshake, Aunt Clarissa gave me her rough cheek to kiss, Uncle Miles congratulated me effusively on getting the scholarship, but nothing was said about the letter until the pudding was finished and Thorne was out of the way. Lady W no longer came down to dinner, and although Stephen had not taken her place at the end of the table there was a distinct change in his attitude, not to me particularly but in the way that he did such things as ringing the bell or pouring out the wine. He had always done these things deferentially, now he did them as of right. He took the decanter of port from the sideboard, poured some into Clarissa's glass and then into his own, and said: "No answer. It seems to have done the trick."

Miles twiddled his glass. "I wouldn't be too sure."

"It needed a little firmness, that's all."

"And the money," Miles said.

"If you ask me the money was a mistake." Clarissa drank half her glass and thumped it back on the table, as she always did. "A great mistake."

The decanter had come round to me. It had been established twelve months ago that I might have the ration of one glass, no more, no less. I poured it now, and looked at the red liquid. I felt Stephen staring at me.

"You don't know what we're talking about, do you? Or has she shown you the letter?"

"I've seen it," I said. "And I've talked to Peterson. I know you've written to—to the man. But I don't know about any money."

I felt hostility in the way they looked at me, even Miles with whom I had always been friendly, and I could understand something of what they must be feeling. Stephen and Miles were Wainwrights, and Clarissa was one by marriage. I was an interloper, brought here for no better reason than the whim of an old woman. But when the silence was broken by Miles' voice, he sounded as friendly as ever.

"Well, then, that saves us a lot of explaining. You see, Stephen wrote and told this fellow that if he came over here or pestered Mamma any further, he'd really be in trouble. It was done to scare him off, and it's done just that. And at the same time, this is what Clarissa was talking about, he sent the man twenty-five pounds."

"I see," I said, although I did not see at all. "You think, then, that the letter isn't from David."

"From David!" Stephen got up, pushed back his chair and began to walk about the room. His eyes, dark like his mother's, but small and intense where hers were large and lustrous, stared at me. "Of course it's not from David, David died in the war. Don't you understand that this sort of thing is the commonest kind of confidence trick when a woman's lost her son, don't you know that?"

"Just why I was against giving him money," Clarissa said, evidently continuing a long argument. "Give it 'em once, they come back again. Twenty-five quid's not bad pay for a begging letter."

"There is no question that this letter is a forgery, no question, do you understand?" Stephen went out of the room, almost ran in his eagerness, and came back with a letter which he put before me. The date was 1941, the letter began "Dear Stephen" and was signed "David." "The writing is quite different, you can see that."

"Yes, it does look different." I went on half-apologetically, "This letter's signed David."

"Well?"

"The other one is signed Rikki Tikki."

Stephen turned away impatiently. Miles said, "That was the name Mamma used for David."

"I know that. How did this man know it?"

The three began to speak together, and then Miles held up a hand. Like Stephen, he seemed anxious that I should believe what he was saying.

"Use your common, my old Christopher. David's plane was shot down, there's no doubt he was killed. But say that this chap was someone in his squadron, a friend of his even. There are a dozen different ways he could have known about the name. Maybe he saw David writing letters, maybe he was a censor, perhaps he saw a letter from Mamma that began 'Dear Rikki'." Miles beamed and mopped his red brow. Stephen broke in.

"The important thing is that this was the only bit of

identification. The rest is the sort of stuff anyone could have made up."

They were curiously anxious to convince me, I thought, and then something else occurred to me. "But she's expecting him. She told me so."

Clarissa slapped her thigh with her palm, almost as though her hand were a riding crop. "You'd better tell him."

"She's written to him." There was silence. "So he'll write back to her."

Miles did not look at me. Stephen gave me a glance, then looked away. It was Clarissa, always impatient of fine feelings and subtleties, who spoke. "Come on, come on. What's done is done." To her husband she said, "What's done is right."

Stephen gave her an uneasy look and I realised, as I had never done before, that behind the stiffness and starch he was a weak man. She turned to Miles and then, seeing that he too would say nothing, back to me. "For God's sake, are you frightened of the boy? He's got to know." She spoke to me directly, her thick neck reddening with the words. "She did write to him, but Peterson took the letter. We told her to. We destroyed it. And if he writes another letter to her, we shall make sure she doesn't get it."

For a moment I could not take it in and then, looking at Miles and Stephen a little shamefaced, and Clarissa with her lower lip out-thrust like one of her own dogs, I knew that it was true. "You can't do that," I said.

"Oh, can't we?" That was Clarissa.

Miles interjected something about trying to understand, but I ignored him. When I thought of that poor old woman upstairs I felt angry.

"No. I shan't let you." I stood up, and knocked over the little that was left in my glass of port. It stained the cloth, but none of them so much as glanced at it. They were watching me. "I expect you're right about the letter. But to do it this way, to let her write to him and expect to see him when she never will—" I couldn't find words for what I thought about it. "I shall tell her."

I had begun to move towards the door, but my way was blocked by Stephen. He came towards me with creeping steps, his white face distorted with hatred. "*You* will tell her. Do you understand your position in this house, do you know that nobody wanted you here, that Mamma simply took you in out of pity, do you know that?"

"Go on," I said.

"You have been fed and clothed and sent to school at our expense, and now you have the audacity to tell us the way in which to behave to Mamma. If she were told the truth it would kill her, do you understand. If you tell her and she dies—" For a moment I thought he was going to spit at me, then he turned away.

Uncle Miles rubbed a hand over his head in embarrassment. I knew that he hated scenes. "Don't be hasty, Christopher, try to understand."

This is all ridiculous, I thought, it belongs to Victorian melodrama. When Uncle Miles asked me to think about it I said I would, but that it would make no difference. I did not want to prolong the argument, and in my hurry to get to the door tripped over a rug before I reached it. My exit was hardly a glorious one.

Chapter Three
The Coming of the Claimant

In the morning things always look different, and on this particular morning the scene of the previous night seemed more than ever ridiculous. Belting was the kind of house where at night it was easy to believe in machinations of a good old-fashioned kind, wills hidden in the secret drawers of desks, the return of the long-lost heir, even cupboards and passages leading from one room to another. In daytime, on a fine July morning, such thoughts seemed absurd. I drew the curtains, got back to bed, propped up the pillows behind my head, and looked around the room, pleased with what I saw. Lady W had agreed that my Thomas Lovell—which was the name I had invented for my bedroom based on a word fantasy worthy of Uncle Miles (I had once called the bedroom "beddoes," Beddoes was a poet, drop the surname and you have his Christian name Thomas Lovell left)—might be done over to my own taste, and I had had the walls covered with a Japanese grass paper, against which I had put Hokusai prints, some Chinese wall mats, and several drawings by a modern Japanese primitive who had lost his reason and committed suicide at the age of twenty-three. Dotted around the room were bits of Japanese pottery. There was a lacquered desk at which I sometimes wrote poems, and a lacquered table with a chessboard top at which I worked out chess problems. I dare say these may sound incongruous accompaniments for a bedroom which contained also an old-fashioned washstand and an uncompromisingly Victorian brass bed. I can only say that at the time I got great pleasure from it.

I meditated for a while in my Thomas Lovell, and came to the conclusion that I had probably been rather silly. No doubt Stephen and Miles were doing what they thought best for Lady W, it would be wrong even to think anything else, and it was not for me to criticise them. I felt the force of this, although I was still determined that in some way or another Lady W must learn that the letter was a hoax. She was the kind of tough old lady who would always prefer the truth, however much pain it might cause her, to an easy lie, and if her sons had not been so much afraid of her they would have realised that. If necessary I would tell her myself, as I had said. With this settled in my mind I got up, washed and spoke aloud two lines of a poem by somebody or other that had got stuck in my mind:

> *What shall we talk of, Li-po, Hokusai,*
> *You narrow your long eyes to fascinate me.*

I narrowed my own eyes in a fairly hideous Victorian looking-glass, looked out at the bright morning, and went downstairs in a good temper. In the breakfast-room I found Clarissa and Uncle Miles—Uncle Stephen had already gone to his Folkestone office—and it seemed that they too were anxious to forget last night's scene. Clarissa was tucking into a great mound of scrambled egg at considerable speed, in the intervals of making telephonic arrangements for the vet to come and have a look at a couple of the dogs, sorting out notes for a talk she was to give to the Women's Institute called "Getting the Best out of the Breed," and arranging about lunch with one of the dailies who also did some cooking. Uncle Miles greeted me cheerfully, gave me one of his winks when Clarissa was not looking, and returned to consideration of the *Daily Worker*, which he took because he said they had the best racing correspondent in the country. Racing and cricket were Uncle Miles' chief interests. Everything seemed to have returned to normal, even to Uncle Miles' slightly furtive extraction from his pocket of a small book in which he began to make pencilled calculations, calculations that would, I knew, turn into elaborate doubles, trebles, and accumulators, rather than simple win or place bets.

Later I tried to see Lady W, but Peterson told me that she never saw anybody in the mornings now, because it was not her best time. Uncle Miles had disappeared, and the yelping of dogs told me of Clarissa's whereabouts. I did not mind being alone. For the first day or two of the holidays I liked simply to luxuriate in being back at Belting, I sank back into the delicious country idleness of life there. I took Max Beerbohm's *Works* and went out into the garden. Almost at the door I met old Thorne.

"Just a minute, Mr Christopher." I stopped, and he seemed uncertain how to go on. "Is there any truth in what I'm hearing, that Mr David's alive and he's coming back?"

There the question was, and what could I say? I tried to equivocate. "Who told you that?"

"Marley, he does a bit of gardening you know, said Miss Peterson told him. Said she had it from her ladyship."

Thorne and Peterson were barely on speaking terms. I made what seemed to me an adroit reply. "As far as I know there's no truth in it."

"Because if Mr David's coming back he wants to watch out for himself. There'll be trouble."

I stared at him. "What do you mean?"

"You won't remember, no more will Mr Miles very like. But he wants to think about it. There'll be trouble."

Thorne's nose was bent very much to one side, a fact that gave him a misleadingly crafty expression. I asked again what he meant, but he shuffled away muttering. Later, when Uncle Miles appeared, I asked him too.

"Don't know what he's talking about. I sometimes think old Thorne's brain is going a bit soft. But since there's no question of David's appearance it's what's called an academic point. Meaning, a bit of nonsense."

I said awkwardly—boys don't find apologies easy—"I'm afraid I made a fool of myself last night."

He beamed. "Stephen didn't do so badly either."

"I'm going to apologise to him. After all, he's old—"

"He's a year older than I am."

"I shouldn't have spoken to him like that. But I still feel Lady W ought to be told what you've done. She's tough enough to take it."

Uncle Miles smiled so often that it was strange to see how his mouth turned down, how sombre he looked, when he was serious. "Yes, I can see you would feel that. Leave it till this evening, and we'll talk it over with Stephen. I promise there'll be no fireworks tonight." He smiled, and it was as though the sombre look had been sponged away, so that the Uncle Miles I knew could return. "Is your name Dennis?"

"What?"

"Because I really came out to say 'Tennis, Dennis.' Meaning to say that you ought to be able to beat an old man by Miles."

"I can only reply like the boy who was asked by his teacher if he could say what was Napoleon's nationality."

"What was that?" Uncle Miles asked incautiously. "He said 'Of course I can' and got top marks."

These jokes look enormously silly put down on paper, but they were the sort of thing that amused Uncle Miles, and in those days they amused me too. It seems ridiculous to say that from the time I came to Belting Uncle Miles had been my best friend, when he was more than double my age, but I can't find any better way of putting it. That evening when he got down on the floor and played with the mechanical bowler was only the first of many. He had a passion for all sorts of adolescent games from l'Attaque and Buccaneer to the sort of indoor cricket that you play on paper by picking words out of a book. I remember finding in his room one day a complete record of a series of Test matches between England and Australia, in which the England team were the actual players of those days, Hutton, Compton, Bedser and the others, with the addition of M Wainwright, who did remarkably well with both bat and ball. I had just reached the age at which I was beginning to find Uncle Miles' make-believe absurd, but unlike most day dreamers he was quite a useful cricketer and tennis player in real life. Now, when we got our rackets and played on the old hard tennis court, he was delighted when he beat me. Afterwards we went and sat by the strippling ream—and now I have brought my narrative up to the point I had reached on the first page, and high time too, you may think.

Why did I feel embarrassed about that Max Beerbohm quotation, the one in which he said at the age of twenty-three that he would write no more? Well, during my six years at Belting I had learned a good deal about Uncle Miles, both from other people and from what he had told me himself, and I could see that the remark might have a personal application.

I knew that at Oxford Uncle Miles had been one of the stars of the OUDS, that against his father's wish he had insisted on making the stage his career, and that he had never done much good as an actor. Then there was something about a marriage that had broken up, although I didn't know the details. On the grand piano there was a photograph of Miles, looking gay and eager, and with a fine thatch of dark hair. It was impossible for me to recognise in this photograph the little bald man I knew, whose mouth turned down at the corners, who played a cunning game of tennis, was devoted to county cricket, and spent an hour a day in placing bets on horses. But the chief reason for embarrassment was Uncle Miles' novel. At the age of twenty-two he had published a novel called *On the Road to Roundabout*. There was no proper library at Belting, but books were to be found in almost every room, in no discernible order, and I had discovered a copy of Uncle Miles' novel one day in, of all places, the Pam Moor. It was one of those light, bright, slight novels about nothing very much that young men published between the wars. Of course, he found me reading it.

"Thought I'd got rid of all those," he said, and gave his occasional deprecating giggle. "Know how many copies it sold? A hundred and eighty-nine. What do you think of it? Don't say, I can tell from the look on your face. Know what the reviewers said, the four who noticed it? They all said 'promising.' You can't have a deadlier word than that, young Christopher, it's the kiss of death. I never wrote anything else."

You can see why it was a maladroit quotation from Beerbohm. But Uncle Miles did not seem to be upset by it. He said, to himself as much as to me, as he sat staring across the stream, "You don't know what the Wainwrights are really like, do you? Or what Mamma's like?" I lay on my stomach and listened. "She's a remarkable woman, no doubt about that, but she never had any life outside the family, never wanted any of us to go away. And none of us did, until the war took us away."

"I thought Hugh started his own business."

"So he did, but where did he do it? Folkestone. And he went on living here."

"What were they really like, Hugh and David?"

"They weren't like what Mamma may have told you. Hugh was tough in a sort of way, and he was always talking about what he was going to do, but he never did it. Did she tell you he wrote plays?"

"Yes."

"So he did, but I'll bet she didn't tell you what they were like. He was dotty about Ibsen, and these plays were Ibsen and water. No producer would look at them, and I don't wonder. Of course Mamma insisted that he was a misunderstood genius, but I don't think she really ever believed it herself. It was David who was the apple of her eye, he was so handsome. Hugh was pretty wild."

"How do you mean?"

"He had all sorts of bright ideas that were going to make a fortune. One was to charter a lot of river boats which he was going to buy cheaply and rent out during the summer. Another was some sort of patent de-ruster. Another was a racing system, something to do with backing second favourites." Uncle Miles snorted, with the contempt of a man who has tried all racing systems, "And what did he turn out to be? An estate agent, and he was no good at that, when he died they found out the firm was bankrupt and it had to be closed down." His voice had become slightly shrill.

"What about David? You say he was the one Mamma really liked." It was always a slight effort to me to say "Mamma".

"David was a charmer, it's true, but he never did anything either. Very shy, and then when he'd got over the shyness he'd be—flippant, I suppose you'd call it. Went to art school, but he wasn't much good. Then he wrote poems and sent them to little magazines. A few of them were printed, and of course Mamma was in the seventh heaven over that, but it never amounted to anything. He and Hugh were very close, he relied on Hugh in lots of ways." Uncle Miles turned towards me, and on his little red face there was the pain of talent unacknowledged. "Mamma's told you they were both geniuses, I dare say. Take it from me, Christopher, they weren't. Hugh was good company, talked a lot, got on well with people. David was a kind of shrinking violet, tremendously sensitive and all that, but what did either of them ever *do*? Nothing. I was the only one who ever did anything, ever published a book. And I was the only one who got away from home, too. Even if I was never a good actor, I did get away. I only came back after Hugh and David died. Mamma wanted me to, and it seemed I ought to. I thought I should be able to come back just for a few weeks, but I never got away again. She eats you up, you know. She eats you up."

There was bitterness in his voice now. I was uncomfortable, because I had never known him like this. "What about your father?"

"He was never much interested. Four sons, and not one a professional soldier. Anyway, Mamma swamped him too."

"Uncle Miles. Why would it be such a catastrophe if he—this man—if he were David? I know he's not," I added hurriedly. "But supposing it were true, why should you and Stephen be so upset?"

Far, far away a small car beetled in off the main road, and began to crawl along the drive. Uncle Miles pulled up some bits of grass, put a couple of pieces in his mouth. "I've made a mess of things," he said. "But it's not all been my own fault. I want something back out of it."

"What do you mean?"

"Money." With an attempt to regain his usual flippancy he said, "To be frank about it, young Christopher, filthy lucre. When Mamma dies Stephen gets the house, you get your whack, old Thorpe and Peterson get something and so on, but there'll be a tidy sum for me. I don't know how much, but—well, a tidy sum. Now, supposing David came back, what do you think would happen, who d'you think would get the house then?"

"I see."

"Horrible old Muncle Iles with his eye on the chain mance," he said. "That's what you think. But it isn't quite like that. I've earned my inheritance, Christopher, and I want it."

"I suppose so." He was right, it did seem to me horrible to be concerned with money in that way. I liked Uncle Miles, but what he was saying now seemed to me disgusting.

The beetle car clattered across the cattle grid and turned into the drive of pollarded yews that led up to the courtyard in front of the house.

"If I could have my time over again—" Uncle Miles said. The beetle stopped in the courtyard and two men got out. He got to his feet. "What's that?"

"Probably the vet to see Clarissa."

"It's not the vet," he said quite sharply. He began to walk with his springy, slightly hurried step, towards the house. I followed him more slowly. As he neared the house Uncle Miles broke into a trot, holding the panama hat on to his head with one hand. I trotted too, rather ridiculously, after him.

As we came past the tennis court and on to the gravel I saw the two men properly for the first time. One was hook-nosed, tall, dressed with a sort of spurious elegance in a suit that gave the impression of being too small for him. He looked at the front of the house, then at his companion, then at Uncle Miles, with a perpetual small smile in which there was something uneasy. But it was at sight of the other man that a shiver went up my back as though the day were cold, for I knew without anything being said that it was he who had written the letter from Paris. He was just above medium height, and he carried himself with a natural grace that contrasted with his companion's uneasiness. He wore an old and shabby blue suit and his face was worn and lined, but when he looked at us, as he did now at Uncle Miles and me standing beside him, I saw or thought I saw the boyish seriousness on the face of the photograph on the grand piano. He stepped forward with his hand outstretched and said, in a voice that was easy and pleasant with a ripple of laughter beneath it, "If it's not old Miles, looking all hot and bothered at sight of me. Miles, old chap, how are you?"

Uncle Miles retreated a step, as though the outstretched hand was the reared head of a poisonous snake. His voice was hoarse as I had never heard it as he said, "What sort of game is this?"

"Oh, come on now, Miles, I haven't changed that much." He turned to me and said, "And who are you?"

"My name's Christopher Barrington. I'm—"

"You'll be the son of, let me think, of Jimmy Barrington and old Jonathan's daughter, right? I'm David Wainwright." He grasped my hand. "And this is my friend Silas Markle.

Markie, meet Christopher Barrington and my brother Miles. I'd know Miles anywhere, although he doesn't seem to be so sure of me at the moment."

The hook-nosed man bobbed his head and said something, and then two things happened. A little way behind the visitors stood a number of topiary birds, and from a ladder just behind one of these descended in an uncertain manner old Thorne. At the same time Clarissa turned the corner of the house that led to the stables, three bull terriers in tow on leads.

"Mr David," Thorne said. "It is you, then, you've come back to us." He advanced upon the stranger, who clasped him warmly, while the old man repeated over and over, "I knew you'd come back, I always said you'd come back."

Clarissa approached. If there had been uncertainty about Miles, there was none in her. She recognised the enemy immediately. "You wrote that letter," she said, and there could be no mistaking the hostility in her voice.

The stranger disentangled himself from Thorne. "You'll be my sister-in-law Clarissa. We haven't met before, but I must give myself the pleasure of greeting a new relative."

"Just try it and I'll set Brush and Bounce on you." At mention of their names the bull terriers snarled appreciatively or threateningly. The stranger took a couple of steps towards her, then stopped and said rather lamely, "Not what I'd call a friendly reception, eh, Markle?"

Clarissa stood square as a stone. I never liked her, but I almost admired her at that moment. "You had our letter, Mr Stiver or whatever your name is. You got your money, though you'd have had none if I'd had my way. Now you're here for more. I can tell you there's nothing doing. You and your friend can get back in that car and go back where you came from, do you understand? I'll count ten, and if you're not in the car and driving away by then I shall set the dogs on you. Believe me, you'll wish you'd got in the car if I do."

The stranger looked at Markle, Markle shrugged his lean shoulders slightly, and I don't know what might have happened then, had the situation not been totally changed by a diversion. A moment before I had heard the sound of a window opening, but had been too absorbed in the scene before me to look round. I think Uncle Miles had been the only one looking towards the house, for he raised and dropped his hand in a hopeless gesture at the same moment that Lady W called from the open window: "David. David, my boy."

She was there at the window, her white hair wild and her arms like two long sticks outstretched, and it was as though her voice had broken a spell. The stranger cried joyously, "Mamma," ran to the house and disappeared within the entrance hall. Clarissa looked for a moment as if she would release the dogs regardless of the fact that Lady W was watching, and then marched over to Miles and snapped that he should hold the dogs. When he asked where she was going, she flung over her shoulder the words that she was going to telephone Stephen. Thorne also had made his way towards the house, no doubt to spread the news. Markle, who had not spoken, now took out a cigarette case and offered its contents to Miles, who refused with an angry shake of the head, and then to me. When I also refused he snapped the case decisively shut and said, "We may as well go in. Cooler indoors than out. Will you lead the way, young man?" There was something unpleasant, in the tone rather than the words, but still there seemed nothing for it but to go into the house. I left Uncle Miles tugging away at the dogs' leads, trying to get them round to the stables. They were waiting for their mistress.

Chapter Four

Dinner and Afterwards

I shall never forget dinner that evening. Lady W came down to it, came down with her hair restored by Peterson, not quite into its old pyramidal elegance it is true, but still looking marvellously fresh. Nothing could make her appearance now anything but gaunt and beaky, but cosmetics had given her cheeks the illusion of health, and her eyes blazed as though a little fire had been lighted inside them. She did not look well, but there was a vivacity about her that it was disturbing to see. It seemed even to disturb David (I had better call him that now, since Lady W had accepted him immediately as her son). She was at the head of the table and he sat on her right hand. Again and again she leaned over to touch him, the touch being made to emphasise a point or to ask a question. It seemed to me that these touches, and the very animation with which she talked to and at him, made him uneasy. When he looked at her and spoke to her he seemed nervous, whereas the few remarks he addressed to Stephen and Miles were made with a jaunty assurance that obviously infuriated them. The brothers said very little during dinner. Stephen, at the other end of the table, opposite Lady W, watched David as though he grudged every piece of food that went into his mouth. Once or twice I thought he would burst out and denounce his "brother" as a fraud, but if he thought of doing so an exchange that took place early on must have checked him.

"You are a very naughty boy, Rikki," Lady W said coquettishly, just touching his arm and drawing back.

"Why?"

"Not answering my letter, just arriving like this. If I'd known, I should have made proper preparations."

There was silence. David glanced at Markle, then looked directly at Stephen and I knew that he guessed what had happened, that Lady W's letter had never been posted and that Stephen was responsible. Stephen ran a hand inside his collar and waited, with a piece of meat on his fork. Then David said, lightly, gaily, "I'm a bad hand at writing letters, Mamma, you know that, and when I had the chance of coming over I just came."

"And now you're here, you'll stay?"

He looked at her, but the words seemed to be spoken to us all. "If you'll have me."

The rest of us said little. Uncle Miles only picked at his food, and Stephen did the same. Clarissa, who sat opposite David, was a powerful trencherwoman and she champed through the meal as usual, giving David an occasional glare to which he responded with a bright smile. Markle, next to her, was watchful, his gaze flickering from one person to another as though he were all the time assessing reactions. And I, what did I feel? I watched what was happening as though it were a comedy being played out before me. I realised that Stephen and Miles were silenced by fear that David would reveal details of the letter they had sent, and still more by concern about the letter of Lady W's that they had intercepted. Since I had felt indignant at the shabby trick they had played, I was pleased that they were hamstrung. I did not question that the stranger was David, for a mother must surely know her own son, but still there was something about Markle, and about the way in which David had let his brothers know that he held the whip hand, which made me uneasy.

With dinner over, fruit was put on the table. David selected an apple and peeled it, beginning at the centre. Lady W exclaimed happily.

"Still just the same, beginning at the centre. I've never seen anyone do it quite like that."

"Still the same. I'm unique." He cast a quick, amused glance round the table.

"You promised upstairs that you'd tell us—" Lady W said, again coquettishly, almost as though she were a little girl asking to be told a bedtime story. Beneath the rouge her cheeks were waxen.

"My dreary history, yes. That is, if you're sure you want to hear it." Again the quick glance round.

"Of course we want to hear. We want an explanation." That was Stephen, and Clarissa added in a tone far from friendly, "You don't meet a new brother-in-law every day."

"Don't we still have a glass of port?" When David had filled his glass he began to talk, and as he told his story the constraint he had shown at dinner fell away, and he talked with an ease and fluency he had not shown since the few minutes after his arrival.

"I don't know how far back I ought to go. Let's begin at the beginning. You know when I was posted missing, in a raid on the synthetic oil plants in the Ruhr. Hell of a night, hell of an operation. Too much low cloud for Mosquitoes to mark the target as they were supposed to, but visibility above cloud was very good, just what the doctor ordered for Jerry fighters. We lost more than twenty kites and mine was one of them, right? Missing, believed killed. Well, I wasn't." David took a sip of port. There was no doubt that he had our attention.

"By rights I should have been killed. We were shot up by two Jerry fighters, Blakeney the navigator and Copp the gunner were killed, and two others were hit. We can't have been more than a few hundred feet from the ground when we parachuted out. I don't know what happened to the others, there was a lot of flak about, very likely they were shot before they reached the ground. I was in luck. I landed with a broken arm, decided I might as well give myself up, knocked on the door of the nearest house a few minutes' walk away. The man was a mine foreman, a Socialist, fed up with the war. He and his wife took me in, kept me in a room until my arm was better, got me a fake German passport. Then Hans, that was the miner's name, arranged to get me on a lorry going down south. I was crated up as some sort of machinery, and Hans put in food and drink to last me for a couple of days. The idea was I would get into occupied France and try to contact the resistance groups there, and Hans had given me some names. But that was the point at which my luck ran out. The lorry went south all right, but it went to Hungary, which as you may remember was on the skids at that time. The driver must have taken some sort of wrong route, because they ran slap into the Russians. The Russians decrated me, but they wouldn't believe I was British, or what was I doing with a German work permit? I believe they came to the conclusion that I was some sort of German spy trying to get information. Anyway they sent me to this labour camp, Novoruba. I'm talking too much."

"Oh, no," Stephen said. "We're very interested."

I looked at Lady W to see if she had taken in the malice of Stephen's tone, but she was sitting back in her chair with eyes half-shut. I could not even be sure that she was listening to David.

"Novoruba—I don't really want to talk much about that. I was there for years, I don't know how many. Eight years, I suppose, something like that. We lived in huts, sixty to a hut, with one small stove to keep us warm in winter. Deaths were something like twenty per cent a year. One day after an old man had died, he was a Pole and he simply died of cold and semi-starvation, I asked for an interview with the camp commander. I got it, which was a pity. He asked what I wanted and when I told him I had a complaint he listened to it. I lost my temper a bit, and said the Russians were in every way worse than the Germans. That put him in a towering rage. He shot off a whole stream of Russian I couldn't understand, and then I was hiked outside and frogmarched away in a direction away from our hut. I told them I wanted to go back, and when they took no notice I punched one of them in the guts and started to run. That was a mistake because I never had a hope. When they caught up with me, two or three of them whanged me on the head very thoroughly with the damned great wooden staves they carried. One of them also did a nice job of stamping on my hand and breaking some bones in it. Nobody bothered whether they mended properly, and they didn't. That's why my writing isn't what it was."

He held up his right hand. Two of the fingers were much shorter than the others, and the whole hand was bunched together and contorted like the hand of a sufferer from arthritis. His cheek twitched, his face was heavy with brooding.

"I can remember every detail of life in the camp, but I can't distinguish one day from another, one year from another even. I'll tell you what I remember. Breakfast. Every day it was a sort of soup, either thin with bits of gristle or stiff with some kind of filthy coarse lentil. Then bread, disgusting uneatable bread that gave you dysentery. Sometimes a bit of sausage as a treat. Rock sausage we used to call it, because one day somebody broke a tooth on it. Then we worked all day, we were supposed to be constructing some kind of dam I think. I had to work even when my hand was healing. Afternoon meal, or dinner or whatever you call it, was the same as breakfast except that sometimes you got a few vegetables in the soup." He shuddered, and the violence of it went all through his body.

"I can't—I can't talk about it much, I've tried to forget it. They treated us like animals, and in the end you turn into an animal if you're treated that way. There were exceptions. Some of the guards were decent. I remember one of them, a boy whose name I could never pronounce. I called him Ivan. He always used to be slipping us cigarettes or bits of chocolate, I don't know where they came from or what would have happened to him if he'd been caught. Two or three times I thought about trying to escape, and once I tried it when Ivan was on duty. I began to work farther and farther away from the rest of them, and from Ivan too. When I was out of sight of everybody I began to think that Felix, he was a Rumanian who always claimed that escaping was easy though he never tried it himself, was right. And then Ivan suddenly appeared. He shook his head at me and pointed to the plains all around us, flat as a pancake and said, '*Niet.*

Nix. No good.' When he said this he pointed to his tongue and I understood, what I'd known all along really of course. Since I spoke only a few words of Russian how the hell could I escape? That was a bad evening, I can tell you." He drank the rest of his port. "They let me go, let a whole lot of us go, quite suddenly, just sent us across and dumped us in West Germany. And they gave me back my fake German work permit. I worked my way across Germany, and into France, then hitched a lift to Paris. And why didn't I tell you I was alive, why didn't I come straight back?" He seemed to ask himself this question. Lady W, to whom he had been talking almost as if the rest of us were not there, was leaning back in her chair, the red spots on her cheeks conspicuous now as the skin beneath them showed yellower. Markle had lighted a cigar, and was puffing away at it. The rest of us were silent.

"I don't know that I can give a single answer, a simple answer that is. Remember how I always wanted to live in Paris, Mamma, when I was studying art, and I never did? Here was the chance. I had no money, I had to get a job, and in the last year I've had half a dozen, porter at a hotel, clerk in a shipping office, waiter in a café. Hard life, I've had enough of it. That was one thing. But the other, the chief reason, was that when I came out of the camp I couldn't think of myself as a human being. I didn't feel it was possible to come home, face up to all of you, to English life. I wasn't ready for it."

"But you're ready now?" Uncle Miles asked. He sat with the corners of his mouth turned down disapprovingly. Lady W looked at him. David nodded, and then shrugged.

"I don't know. I hope so. You've got to understand what it was like in the camp to be able to realise what I felt. You're—degraded, degraded by the sort of things that happen to you, the things you do yourself. You get to a point at which the only thing you're fit for is the lowest, most mechanical work, the only people you want to be with are scum, the sort of stagnant scum you don't find in ordinary society. I used to think that Russian writers were exaggerating things, but not long ago in Paris I read Dostoevsky's *House of the Dead*, and my God, it's true enough. Life in Russia—they live like pigs and dream about heaven. Am I making sense? I can't help it if I'm not. When I got to Paris I felt I couldn't face English life, and then a couple of weeks ago—" He stopped.

"Yes," Stephen said. "What happened a couple of weeks ago?"

"I took an overdose. The chap who ran the wretched little hotel I was in found me all right, perhaps I never meant to take a lethal dose, but I knew then it was no good. It was then I wrote to you, Mamma."

Lady W sat up in her chair, opened her eyes wide. "I shall go to bed. Rikki, your old room is ready for you. Mr Markle, you'll stay here, of course."

Markle took his cigar from his mouth. "Very kind of you, Lady Wainwright, but I shouldn't think of imposing. I've already booked a room at the Rising Sun."

As Lady W stood up she swayed a little. David was at her side in a moment. "The excitement. A little too much for me. It's nothing."

"I'll come upstairs with you."

"Yes. And then if you'll tell Peterson." The smile she gave us was ghastly. She went out of the room leaning heavily on David's arm. The door had barely closed when Stephen said in his thin, acid voice, "Now, Mr Markle."

Markle stubbed out his cigar and smiled at Stephen, who said, "Why are you here?"

"I'm a solicitor. Steinberg, Markle and Fasnach. I'm here to look after Mr Wainwright's interests."

"You know that we dispute his identity," Clarissa bayed at him.

"Your husband wrote a letter to that effect. I have it in my possession. He offered my client money, which of course we shall return."

We had sat a long while at the dinner table and now Susan, the maid who had helped to serve the meal, came in, not for the first time. As we were going through to the drawing-room Markle excused himself, saying that he had some papers in the car that might interest us. He came back briskly cheerful, with a briefcase under his arm which he unzipped. I looked at the things it contained with a curiosity which may be imagined, and ended my inspection rather disappointed.

The things he put upon a table were a copy of Donne's *Songs and Sonets*, bent at the edges and obviously much read, and a tattered wallet. In the manner of a lecturer he described them. "This little book was given to my client by Mr Miles Wainwright. There is an inscription inside the front cover." There was, too: *David from Miles, Christmas 1943*. "You don't dispute that this is the copy you gave him?"

"I don't dispute it."

"Good, good. We're making progress. Now, this is the wallet he had during the war. You may recognise it? No? Well, this is the one. Contents, pay book, letters. One here from Lady Wainwright, one from his brother Hugh, one from a lady friend named Joyce. A few other odds and ends, like this small key with a lion's head on it, perhaps you recognise that? Well, there you are, gentlemen."

"These don't mean anything," Stephen said. "They could have been taken off David's body."

At the same time Clarissa asked, "How does he happen to have them still in his possession?"

"A good question, Mrs Wainwright," Markle said, still in his lecturer's rôle. "The Russians took the wallet, let him keep the little book of poems, which you can see was his constant companion in camp. Then when the Russians let him go they handed back his wallet intact."

Silence. Then Stephen said, "As far as I'm concerned these don't prove anything, if that's all he's got to show."

Markle shrugged. "What do you expect? You heard his story, it's a marvel he was able to keep anything at all. His mother knew him at once."

"She believed what she wants to believe."

"That old man in the garden recognised him."

"He'd heard this tale about David being alive."

Markle's mouth curved in a sneer. "You two gentlemen are what might be called interested parties I understand, and Mrs Wainwright too. Perhaps even this young gentleman here."

"That's an outrageous insinuation," Stephen cried.

"Oh, come along now, you won't pretend you didn't want to keep my client away from here. That was your object, wasn't it? To buy him off. On the cheap." Markle sat in a cretonne-covered wing arm-chair with his legs stretched out, odiously at ease, and looked around him with surprise. "This really is a period piece, isn't it? Must say I've never seen a room like it. Might be something out of a film."

Stephen confronted him, trembling with indignation. At this moment David returned, and took in the scene.

"Trouble?" he asked.

I can't convey what a difference I felt in his attitude in the way he spoke that one word. It was as though he were saying, "All right, the fancy talk is over, let's get down to business," or as though he had been wearing a mask at the dinner-table and this had dropped for a moment to reveal his true face. These are not afterthoughts, they are things I thought at the time although I didn't formulate them clearly, and you can dismiss them if you like as the fanciful notions of a literary young man. But it is a fact that I had been completely convinced by the evident sincerity with which he told his story, and that the first moment when I really doubted that he was David Wainwright was when he said in that cheerfully aggressive voice, "Trouble?" I think perhaps he knew that his tone had disconcerted me, for he changed it again in a moment.

For the next hour he sat answering questions from Stephen and Miles, and he did so with remarkable coolness and conviction. They asked him about school, about incidents in their childhood, about servants they had had before the war. He answered nine out of every ten questions at once, and obviously what he said was correct. When he didn't remember something he admitted it. At one point Miles said, "What about Durdle Door?"

"What about it?"

"What happened there? On the cliffs? You were ten and I was seven."

"I don't know."

"If you were David you would know. I got stuck on the cliff. You crawled up and helped me to get to the top. We agreed we wouldn't say anything to anybody about it, and we never did." Spitefully—I had never known Uncle Miles spiteful before—he added, "I don't suppose you even know where Durdle Door is."

That last sentence was a mistake, because if David had been on the hook, now he was off it. He laughed. "Of course I do, it's near where we used to go for summer holidays. About the cliff, honestly, Miles, I don't remember a thing.

Try and be reasonable, old man. It was thirty years ago and I've forgotten a hell of a lot since then. For a while after I got out of Russia there were great yawning gaps so that if you'd asked me then what school I went to, I wouldn't have known. Since then a lot's come back to me, but I know there are still some holes."

"If you were David you'd remember," Miles said obstinately.

Markle had lighted another cigar and now he sat forward in the wing chair, pointing with it. "Remember you were the one who got stuck on the cliff. Maybe that's why you'd be the one to remember, eh?"

He looked about for smiles, but found himself ignored. David went on talking. In the time I knew him I never saw him lose his temper, but now he showed his feelings plainly—or was it that he gave a calculated display of anger?

"As a matter of fact I think you've been pretty unreasonable altogether. If I weren't your brother, how the hell do you think I could have answered half your questions, how would I have known my way about the house? I don't want to harp on it, but that letter you wrote, Stephen—well, I don't imagine it's the sort of letter you'd want people to see."

There was a threat in the words rather than in the way they were spoken, but it struck home to Stephen. He pulled at his collar and said something unintelligible. His white face was twisted so that for a moment I thought that he might cry. Then he walked quickly, almost ran, out of the room. Clarissa followed him.

"I can't say I admire Stephen's taste in wives," David said. Markle laughed. "That doesn't apply to your wife, though, Miles. You haven't married again I suppose?"

These apparently harmless words made Uncle Miles clench

his fists. David said tauntingly, "You don't want to do any-thing silly, Miles. Mustn't have a fracas on my first night back under the family roof."

"You're a scoundrel."

"Oh, come along now. I'm your brother. You remember, the one who rescued you from Durdle Door."

Miles stamped his foot in anger at this mockery, a gesture pettish rather than angry. "Why did you come here? If you don't go away I'll—"

He didn't say what he would do and this uncompleted exit line was comic, or if you liked Miles as I did, pathetic.

That left the three of us in the drawing-room, David and Markle and I, and again I seemed to detect in David a change, this time a sense of relaxation as though a hurdle had been surmounted and a breathing space was possible. As David wandered about the room exclaiming at the odds and ends and knick-knacks he remembered, a papier mâché chair and a frame for an embroidery panel, and as Markle said that he must be getting along or they would lock him out of the Rising Sun, I said casually and with no sense of putting a searching question, "What made you choose that name—Stiver?" I hesitated about adding "Uncle David," and decided against it.

Markle merely raised his eyebrows, but David's head jerked back as if we were boxers, and I had shaken him with an uppercut. "What do you mean?"

What had I meant? "Well, it was a kind of joke I sup-pose, was it? Not having a stiver, that means not having any money. Was that it?"

"Yes, of course." It seemed to me that he accepted this suggestion with relief. "It was a joke. A pretty bad one, you may think, but a joke, that's all."

I don't know why I should have been dissatisfied by this explanation, but the feeling of dissatisfaction stayed with me as David saw Markle out, and then said goodnight to me. I went up to bed, along the corridor that no longer held terrors, with my mind in a whirl. I was in my pyjamas and brushing my teeth when there was a knock on the door.

I do not know who I had expected to see standing there, but I was certainly surprised to see Stephen. He too was in pyjamas and dressing-gown, and I was fascinated to see that his neck, when not confined by a tight collar was white as an asparagus stalk. He looked round at my wallpaper and prints with a dislike which I could see he did not want to express, and it was with a humouring air that he said, "I see, you like this sort of thing, do you?" To this remark I made no reply. He tugged at his dressing-gown and burst out, "You've got to help expose this fraud."

I have made it clear that there was no love lost between Stephen and me, and the effect of this remark was to make me feel immediately more kindly disposed towards David. "Why do you say he's a fraud?"

"It's obvious. Don't you think I'd know if he were my brother?"

"What about the wallet and the book?"

"This man must have taken them off David, or got possession of them in some way."

"And Mamma recognised him."

I knew that it infuriated Stephen to hear me calling Lady W, Mamma. He controlled himself with an effort, and said as he had done before, "She's determined to believe it."

I sat down on the bed. "As a matter of fact I think he may be a fraud too."

He asked me why, but did not seem impressed when I

told him about the name. "I don't believe that idea, about not having a stiver, had occurred to him before. He just accepted it when I suggested it."

"Does it matter?"

"My æsthetic sense tells me there's something wrong about it." I could not resist adding, "You see now that there are advantages in belonging to the Æsthetes' Society."

"What?"

"At school. We burn incense while we worship Oscar Wilde on prayer mats."

This was strictly untrue, but I think Stephen half-believed it. The stalk of his neck bulged with his effort to keep his temper. "Are you willing to help?"

"What do you want me to do?"

"While that man is here I shall not leave this house. The ascendancy he has gained already over Mamma is appalling."

"Uncle Miles is here." Stephen made no reply to this, and I was left to wonder whether he was doubtful of Miles' capacity to deal with David. "I suppose you're afraid that Mamma may change her will."

"If she did, you would be affected too." He stopped again, realising I suppose that this argument was not likely to affect me. He stared at one of the Japanese primitives, and turned away from it with distaste. "Christopher, I know this man is a fraud, and I am going to prove it. Miles and I are agreed that we should both stay here for the moment. We want you to go to London tomorrow and see two people who should be able to help. If you agree, I will write letters to both which you can take along, and I'll telephone and tell them to expect you."

I had already decided to say yes when I asked, "Who are they?"

"One is named Betty Urquhart, the other Vivian Foster."

"Hadn't you better tell me why I'm going to see them?"

He bit off the words reluctantly. "Foster was a great friend of David's. He was a doctor. He's in Harley Street now. Betty Urquhart was—she runs some sort of gallery—she was a friend of David's too."

Something about his tone made me ask, "You mean she was his mistress?"

"Yes, I believe so," he said unwillingly, and with something odd in his glance. When I said that I would go he patted me on the shoulder and said "Good man" two or three times. He was a great one for old-fashioned slang, Uncle Stephen.

Chapter Five

Betty Urquhart and Vivian Foster

So it came about that just before midday the next morning I found myself outside the People's Art Gallery, just off Leicester Square. I had seen Lady W, and told her that I had arranged to go up for the day to see a friend in London. A year ago she might have been annoyed that I was spending a day in London so soon after the beginning of the holidays, but now she was so completely occupied with David's return that she hardly noticed what I was saying. The gaiety and vividness of the previous night had all drained away, and although she was cheerful I thought that she looked dreadfully ill. David and Miles had not appeared by the time I left, Clarissa was with the dogs, and so I was left with Stephen, who was looking even more pinched and near-strangled than usual. He gave me the letters, and said that he would ring both Betty Urquhart and Vivian Foster late in the morning.

"We'll spike this fellow's guns," he said as I left, a phrase which made me decide to add up the number of clichés he used and award myself some sort of prize when I'd reached twenty. It was only on the way to the station that I looked at the letters and saw that they were not only sealed but stuck down at the back with sticky tape, a reminder that Stephen was not simply a comic character but a mean one too.

The door of the gallery clanged as I went in. Nobody appeared, so I walked round looking at the pictures. About half of them were abstracts and the other half were social realist, showing labourers with enormous muscles shifting great lumps of iron, that kind of thing. My own preference at the time was for the neat and finicky. Pretty well the only modern pictures I admired were surrealist paintings done with a fanatical, naturalistic attention to detail, and I didn't like any of these very much. I was trying to decipher one of the artists' names when a voice behind me said, "Yes?"

I turned to be confronted with what seemed at first glance to be a thin young man. Only the first of these adjectives proved accurate, for in fact I faced a woman, wearing paint-stained trousers, who was of the same age as those I counted old, like Stephen and Miles. I had been deceived by the loose smock that concealed the breasts, by the trousers, and by the bronze curls that topped an eager, open face innocent of powder and lipstick. "You must be Christopher Barrington. I'm Betty Urquhart."

"How do you do?"

"I do pretty well. I see you've been properly brought up. What do you think of Destrello? You were looking at his paintings."

"I don't like them very much."

"No need to be so bloody cautious, if you think they're no good, say so. He's a genius."

"Is he?"

"So the people who know tell me, but if you think he isn't, there you are. Perhaps you're right."

"Do you work here?"

"Work here? I own the place. I'm promoting Destrello because he's a genius. Smoke?" She sat down behind a small desk, took some canvases off the only other chair and invited me to sit on it. I sat down, but refused the cigarette. I gave her Stephen's letter. She tore it open, read it, struck a match on the heel of her shoe, lighted a cigarette, and made a face. "How do you get on with Stephen?"

"I don't like him much."

"I haven't seen him for years, but he reminded me of a starving crow. I couldn't make head or tail of what he was saying on the telephone, but this letter helps. My God, he's a creep, that Stephen, don't you think so?"

I hesitated, then said, "Yes." We both began to laugh. She opened a drawer, took out half a bottle of whisky, reached behind her and found two small glasses. "Damnation to all creeps."

I had drunk whisky only two or three times before, and didn't really want to now, but I felt that I might label myself a creep if I refused. So I drank damnation to creeps. She put her feet on the desk. "Now, perhaps you'll tell me the truth about all this cock over someone coming along and pretending to be David."

I told her what had happened, about David's return and Lady W's acceptance of him, and his brothers' scepticism. While I talked two or three people came in to look round the gallery. She paid little attention, simply telling them to look around, and handing a price list to a man who asked for it. They had wandered in, as people do in art galleries, and they wandered out again. When I had finished she poured more whisky into both our glasses, and drank half of hers at one gulp.

"I don't get it. What does Brother Creep expect me to do? Why should I care whether it's David or not?"

I hardly knew how to reply. "He thought you might be able to—to say it wasn't David, I suppose."

She swung her legs off the desk. "God Almighty, they're his brothers. If they can't recognise him, how the hell can I?"

"They do. I mean, they don't. They're certain he isn't David."

She stared at me. "Well, then?"

"But they want proof. After all, you were—you had an affair with him." The whisky had gone to my head a little, or I would never have said such a thing. But she was not offended.

"So I did." She paused. "Did Miles know you were coming to see me?"

"I don't know. Does it matter?"

"Perhaps not. But I guess Miles wouldn't have wanted you to come, and Brother Creep kept it from him. And I can see he didn't tell you the whole story. Miles was my husband."

I gaped. She got up, put what was left of the whisky back in the drawer and said, "Drink up. I'll take you out to lunch."

Five minutes later she had yelled to a young man named John to come down and look after the shop, and we were in the first-floor restaurant of a pub called The Fighting Cock, just a few doors away. I should have liked to stay downstairs, where a good many young men in beards were talking to girls who wore jeans, but Betty (she had told me to call her that) said that if we didn't go straight up we wouldn't get a table. She ordered lunch for two, including a bottle of wine. Then she looked at me.

"You're not TT, are you? It's a bit late to ask. So you don't know a thing about Miles and me. Would you like to hear?"

I said yes. It was true enough that I wanted to hear, and I could see that she wanted to tell me.

"Miles was going to be an actor, I was going to be an actress, that's how we met. We both had walking-on parts in a farce that made the West End, then flopped. Miles was young and handsome, anyway I thought so. I was fairly bowled over, I can tell you. Then he took me down to Belting to meet the family, and I stayed the weekend. My God, what a morgue." She saw my look of surprise and distress. "All right, you like it, but you weren't a prospective wife on trial. The old General sized me up as though I were a mare going to stud with a Derby winner, did everything but look at my teeth. He was harmless enough though, in a way I even liked him, it was she who was what you might call the snake in the grass."

"Lady Wainwright?"

"Who else? She's a real vampire that one, sucking the blood of her children, and all of them saying how wonderful she was while she did it. I saw what she was like straight away. I didn't like her, and the feeling was what you might call strongly reciprocated. It made me sick to see the way they all fawned on her."

I echoed the words in surprise. I had not gathered the impression that Hugh or David were likely to fawn on anybody.

"That's what it amounted to. Not so much Hugh, though he never got away from her for all his talk. There they were, stuck in that bloody great barracks of a house pretending to be artists, except Brother Creep of course, Hugh writing his bloody awful plays, David drooping away in a corner thinking up the rhyme scheme for a sonnet, and that old bitch pretending they were all geniuses."

"You knew Hugh as well?"

"Oh, I knew Hugh." She gave me a glance out of the

corner of her eye in which there was something provocative. "After that visit I married Miles."

"They didn't approve?"

"That's putting it mildly. Mind you, I think if I'd said to her that I'd go and live at Belting she wouldn't have said no, because you see Miles was the only naughty boy, the one who wanted to get away. But after that weekend I told him I was never going there again, and if he wanted to marry me we'd do it in a registry office in London. So we did just that, and told them afterwards. There was a row, but there was nothing she could do about it except cut off Miles' allowance. It was the General who wrote the letter, but her fine Italian hand was behind it."

"And then?" I wanted to get on to the affair with David.

"I loved Miles. You know, I really loved that man and in a way I still love him, because he was perfectly sweet, the sweetest man I've ever known."

"I like him too."

"But it never worked out. And why not? The truth is, when I went down to that ghastly place and met the family, I fell hard for Hugh."

"For *Hugh*?" I said in surprise, "But I thought—"

"Yes, I know. I'm coming to that. You're shocked."

There was only one possible answer to that question, and I made it, waving my glass a little as I did so. A little wine spilled on to the cloth. Betty ignored it, and so did I.

"There was something about the way Hugh looked, a sort of boldness—I can't describe it, and you're too young to know what I mean, but it's the kind of signal that sometimes passes between a man and a woman when they meet, and they know they're on the same wave-length if you get me. So there were Miles and I installed in a little flat in Kensington, and Hugh and David would come in to see us sometimes. It made me sick, I can tell you, the way they used to talk about Belting, with Miles lapping it all up. Every so often, while Hugh was saying something to Miles about the old homestead I would catch his eye on me, a sort of look as though he knew I was hating it, and that pleased him. I found it very exciting, can you understand that?" I nodded untruthfully. "And then the day came, and I've always thought Hugh somehow engineered it, when Miles was out and Hugh called."

She paused, looked at me, and went on. "I like sex. To me, you know, having a man is like having a good meal, and you don't always eat at the same restaurant. So loving Miles didn't make any difference, you understand? Oh, damn it, you don't understand, but what does it matter, I don't know why I'm trying to justify myself to you. Anyway, there we were together, and I knew it was going to happen and I wanted it to happen, and Hugh got most of my clothes off, and then do you know what? There I was sprawled on the bed and he was bending over me, and he smacked my face and said, 'Do you think I want Miles' leavings?', and he put on his clothes and walked out." She cocked an eyebrow at me, and then laughed. "What a situation for a girl. They call some girls teasers, but what would you call him? I never saw or heard from him again. Why did he do it, you ask?" (Though I hadn't asked.) "I thought about it a good deal afterwards, and though I should like to think it was my fatal charm that lured him on, I don't think that's true. I think he set out to humiliate me. Deliberately. And I suppose you could say he succeeded. Luckily for me, though, I'm like an india-rubber ball, when I'm hit I bounce back."

"Why should he want to humiliate you?"

"Who knows, Chris? Basically he was queer, I suppose, probably that's why."

"What did Miles think about it?"

"He never knew. Or at least I never told him."

Greatly daring, I said, "What about David?"

She put her chin in her hand and considered David. "He was much more handsome than Hugh, madly good-looking, but in a mother's boy Rupert Brooke sort of way. I'm sure he modelled himself on Rupert Brooke. David went on coming to the flat, even though Hugh didn't, and, well, I told you I was like a rubber ball. I bounced back at David."

I protested. "But you didn't *like* him."

"Oh, I liked him all right in a way, you couldn't help it, he was serious and boyish and brought out the mother impulse that's lurking somewhere in every woman. And then there was another thing. This happened in the early part of the war, David had gone into the Air Force like a patriotic lad, and he was in uniform. I've always gone for uniforms, though of course he wasn't in uniform when we did it." She laughed. "Now I have shocked you."

She had. I bravely said, "Not at all."

"Good for you, even if you don't mean it. Well, as you've gathered, I don't take sex seriously, you enjoy yourself and that's it. But David wasn't like that, he pretty well went crazy. He was stationed not far from London at the time and there were letters, telephone calls, sudden visits. If Miles hadn't been as blind as they come, and working part of the time, he must have known what was going on. As it was, we went on for six months, with David feeling guilty, wanting to tell Miles, weeping round the place, wanting me to get a divorce and marry him, and writing bad poems about it all the time. It was perfect hell for me, I can tell you. I was almost glad when the balloon went up one day, when Miles came home and found us together. There was the most tremendous scene, with Miles and David shrieking at each other like actors in a Jacobean tragedy. I sat back and enjoyed it."

"What happened then?"

"What would you expect? They went home and told their tales to Mamma. I've always thought that she settled it, like an umpire at cricket, you know. Miles and I parted, he took it very hard, and David wrote me reams of letters about how he loved me but we'd better not meet again. I answered one or two, but then I got fed up with them, and just about that time I got tied up with a BBC war correspondent, and—well, that was the end of it. Except that Miles got a divorce. He had plenty of grounds. David wasn't named."

My first reaction was excitement at this glimpse of a sexual bohemianism that I had only read about. Betty Urquhart suddenly appeared to me an entirely different person. What had been a rather old boyish-looking woman in dirty smock and trousers was transformed into an ideal image of sexual freedom. It was hard enough for me to imagine Miles, Hugh and David in the rôles she had allotted to them, but that the first woman who talked to me about having sexual relations with men should wear no make-up and have grubby hands seemed to me almost unbelievable. I drained my glass, and thoughtlessly accepted the brandy she offered. She said abruptly, "I expect you think I behaved badly to Miles."

I had been too thoroughly enthralled to think any such thing, but I said, "Yes."

"I think so too. I was a fool. And I damned well loved Miles, can you imagine that. But you can't help the sort of person you are, can you?"

If this was an appeal to me, I did not answer it. "So Miles hates David."

"You've got it wrong, you don't understand what makes

that family tick. It's all Mamma. Miles wouldn't hate anybody, he's not that kind of man. He wouldn't even hate me. But he was tied to his mother like the rest of them, and when Hugh and David were posted missing he went back to her."

"And David?"

"David was a nice boy, though he had no sense of humour, and could be awfully bitchy at times. Perhaps he's changed."

"But I mean—" I lost track of what I had wanted to say, then rediscovered it. "—I mean, don't you think it's terribly unlikely, David spending a year in Paris before coming home?"

She shook her bronze curls. "Very much in character I should say, making a feeble attempt to get free before going back to Mamma again. Before he started writing bad poems he painted bad pictures, you know that, I expect. What I don't see is how I can help. Even if I wanted to."

"I think what Uncle Stephen's got in mind is that if—I mean, if David's a fake, he won't know who you are from Adam. Eve."

"Uncle Stephen," she said mockingly. "Creeping Jesus. He's married, isn't that so? I can't imagine what sort of woman would marry him."

"Breeds bull terriers, and looks like one."

"It might be fun to see Miles again, at that," she said as she paid the bill.

Out on the street I took in great gulps of air, but they acted on me like so much wine. I found my movements slightly uncertain on the way back to the gallery, and Betty took me by the arm. Her grip was like a man's, strong and firm. The young man, John, raised his eyebrows when he saw us, but said nothing. Betty guided me through a side door, and up some stairs.

"Come on, you'd better sleep it off."

I looked round. I was in a woman's bedroom. I was sitting with Betty on a comfortable bed, with her face inches from mine. It was not her attractiveness that inflamed my senses, but the glimpse she had given me of a world infinitely distant and desirable. I leaned towards her and kissed her, felt the pressure of her breasts against me and her tongue enormous in my mouth. It was too much for me. My eyes closed, and I knew nothing more.

When I opened my eyes again I was alone. My head ached. My shoes and jacket had been taken off. I found a note in the jacket: "Don't have much luck with gentlemen from Belting, do I? Had to go out, back about six. Come to The Fighting Cock for a drink if you're around. Tell Brother Creep I'll come and beard the villain, if he is one. Tomorrow or day after, should be fun. Betty." There was a PS "Why doesn't Creep try family dentist, fillings and all that. I'm sure they had a family dentist."

I lurched downstairs and out. John stared at me with open hostility. I looked at my watch. The time was half past three.

"Yes, I have had a telephone call from your uncle. I couldn't quite understand what he wanted, nor why he didn't come up to London himself." Doctor Foster's gaze took in my youth and my (I dare say) rather wild appearance. It is possible, although I didn't think of it at the time, that he smelt drink on my breath.

I began to explain. We were in his consulting-room, which seemed to be full of black leather furniture. He had said that he could spare me twenty minutes, and I had the feeling that it would not be extended to twenty-one. He sat behind his desk and I was on the other side of it, so that our positions were distinctly like those of doctor and patient. Doctor Foster was a very handsome man. He had dark thick hair beautifully cut and shaped, fine regular features, and long elegant hands. He wore a dark grey suit and a plain white shirt. The cuffs of the shirt shot beyond the jacket arms to reveal emerald cuff links, his one touch of ostentation. He listened to me attentively but with increasing surprise.

"What an extraordinary tale." He played with a paper knife on his desk. "There surely can't be any difficulty in settling whether or not it is David. His handwriting—"

"I said that his right hand is injured."

"So you did."

"Then there's the dentist," I said boldly, using the idea so recently given me by Betty Urquhart. "I believe Uncle Stephen's working on that."

"Yes. There can be little doubt that the man is an impostor."

I took a breath. There was something forbidding, or at least distinctly detached about Doctor Foster. "Suppose he isn't."

"What?" The word was sharply spoken.

"You might be able to help him prove his identity. I mean, he was your best friend, wasn't he?"

"We were friends at Oxford." He got up and went across to the window. "And we were at the same air station for a time during the war," he said as if he were making a concession.

"If there was anything special, any incident that concerned just the two of you—"

"David had an old appendicitis scar, a doctor could check on that. And when he wrote letters to me he used to begin 'Dear Vof'—my second initial is O. I can't think of anyone else who would know that."

The words came readily, yet it seemed to me that in

some way he was evading questions. My head was aching. "Anything else?"

"When David came down—" He stopped and looked at me. "It seems wrong that I should be telling you this, but in view of the letter I suppose there is no harm in it. I left Oxford some time before him, when I decided that I wanted to study psychiatry, and I saw nothing of him in his last year. Then one day I had a telephone call, saying that he wanted to see me urgently. We met in a teashop." He said incredulously, "He wanted to borrow two hundred pounds."

"What for?"

"That was the most outrageous thing about it. For a *gambling debt*. Horse racing. He owed the money to a book-maker."

"Were you able to lend it to him?"

He looked at me as though he would like to commit me to a mental hospital. "It was not a question of being *able* to. I shouldn't do so as a matter of principle."

I reflected that friendship did not go very far for Doctor Foster. "What happened?"

"I had nothing further to do with it, but I believe that David's elder brother Hugh—you've heard of him?"

"Yes."

"I think he saw the bookmaker involved, and induced him to settle for a percentage of the debt. Then he borrowed the money from somewhere. I can only hope the man who lent it got his money back. Hugh Wainwright was far from reliable."

"He seems to have helped his brother."

"And I didn't, is that what you mean? You are too young to understand. I liked David, but he was a spoilt boy, and often behaved like one. People ought to face the consequences of their actions. I thought so then, and I think so now. But there was something else." He said slowly, "I was surprised to learn that David was interested in horse racing. He never had been when I knew him at Oxford. On the other hand, Hugh was always interested, and he had worked out some betting system. It occurred to me that David might have been placing bets for Hugh."

"Why should he do that?"

He coughed. "It is possible that Hugh had—exhausted his credit with bookmakers, shall I say? Anyway, that was a thought that influenced me in making my decision."

Again I sensed some kind of restraint, something that remained unsaid. "Why don't you want to come down?"

He repeated in that sharp tone, "What?" It was not really a question. He came back to the desk, and sat down gingerly. "If it were really David—"

"Yes?"

He made an irritated gesture. "I don't know why on earth they sent you to see me. You're only a boy, you know nothing about it. I suppose Miles may not know either, he was with some ghastly fifth-rate touring company, entertaining the troops." He made it sound as if that were something indecent. "But Stephen was there."

I had no idea what he meant. His secretary, a girl with heavy horn-rimmed spectacles, opened the door. "Mrs Wallbrand is here."

"Tell her to wait." Now the irritated gesture was made in her direction, and she was out of the door in a moment. He touched the grey wings of his hair. "When David went home on his last leave—" He stopped, and began again. "I don't believe he would have come back. If he has, the position may be awkward. For him."

It was very much what Thorne had said, that there would be trouble. "I don't know what you mean, but if you can clear things up you'd better come down, hadn't you?"

He pressed a button on his desk, and the girl with horn-rims came in. "Miss Powers, I shall be going down to the country tomorrow afternoon. What appointments have I got?"

"Three-thirty, Mrs Slade. That's all."

"Fit her in some time the next day. All right. You can tell Stephen Wainwright that I'll come down tomorrow afternoon." He nodded dismissively to show that the interview was over.

I left his rooms in Harley Street seething with anger, a schoolboy who had been put in his place. I suppose I was a schoolboy, but that didn't make it any better, especially after the man of the world, or rather woman of the world, way in which Betty Urquhart had treated me. All the way to Charing Cross I occupied myself by trying to make a variation on "Doctor Foster went to Gloucester." I got no further than "Doctor Foster went to Belting. It was pelting cats and dogs." I read Max to soothe myself all the way back home in the train.

Chapter Six

Murder

There was a little station called Belting Halt only a mile from the house, but few trains stopped there, and I got out at Filehurst, a biggish village which was three miles away by road but half a mile less than that if you went across the fields. I decided to walk back, and crossed a stile just outside the village.

It was a fine evening, and as I walked in the air which had about it the softness and sweetness one often finds in the country after a warm day, I thought about the two people I had seen, and wondered what they would make of the man who said he was David Wainwright. Would Betty Urquhart exclaim immediately, "Go away, you're not the man I slept with," would Doctor Foster order, "Down with your trousers and let's see that scar?", or would they agree with Lady W that this was the man they had known? If I had been asked what I thought myself I should have been puzzled to know what to say. It seemed to me incredible that Stephen and Miles should be uncertain about whether this was their brother—but at that thought I reminded myself that they were not uncertain, they were sure he was an impostor. Put it another way then, could I believe that anybody as shrewd as Lady W would be deceived? I could not believe it really, yet I realised that she was dying and that her intelligence might be blurred. How had David known his way about the house? Well, there might be a dozen explanations for that. But what about all the other things he knew and remembered?

Thinking in this useless and roundabout way I had got about half-way back to Belting when I heard what I took at first to be a human being crying for help, and then knew for the whine of a dog or the cry of a trapped rabbit. I went towards the sound, along a track that led through some bushes, and at a gap in them saw Billy, a puppy that belonged to the house, fidgeting and whining over something partly hidden. When I held aside the bushes I saw that it was a body, the body of old Thorne. He lay very still, there was blood round his head and more blood on his jacket.

The reader of a book like this knows, or immediately suspects, that old Thorne had been murdered, but the much smaller number of readers who have come across a dead body are not likely to have thought of murder as their first reaction, and neither did I. I assumed at once that Thorne had met with an accident, and I pulled his body out of the bushes to see if I could help, Billy yelping at my heels all the while. The puppy was a favourite of Thorne's, who often gave him scraps and protected him from Clarissa's bull terriers. It was after I had pulled him out that I saw the bullet hole in the middle of his forehead, between the eyes. The body was cool to the touch and if I had been able to think rationally I should have known that Thorne had been dead for some time. Instead I foolishly felt for the non-existent pulse, and it was not until I had wasted perhaps a minute that I fully realised that Thorne was dead and that somebody had shot him. As I straightened up from the body I saw that there was blood on my hands. I wiped them as best I could on the grass, and began to run for home. Billy, making a sound that was half-bark and half-whine, followed me.

I ran and trotted all the rest of the way back. The path I had taken led by the stream, the tennis court and, to the side of them, an old disused clock golf green. Here David and Markle were playing. They wore still the clothes they had come down in yesterday and they looked incongruous figures in this English scene, David in his shabby town suit and Markle so obviously out of place in the country, holding the putter as though it were something that might explode in his hands. They turned towards me, David smiling and Markle looking at me with his habitual air of slight super-ciliousness, and their figures set against the green lawn and the stone mass of the house seemed to me for a moment not just incongruous but positively sinister.

"You look in a bit of a tizzy, Christopher," David said. "What's up?"

"Thorne. He's dead. He's been killed." Even now I could not use the word *murdered*.

David's face turned white. He leaned on his putter as though for support, and his mouth moved, but he said nothing. I went into the house, saw Miles and Stephen, and told them. Their reactions were very characteristic. Miles ran a hand over his bald head, his mouth turned down, and he said something about there being no more thorns among the roses. Stephen snapped out four words. As I write them down they seem comic, but I did not think they were comic at the time. "This means the police."

Now Clarissa appeared, with one of the inevitable dogs in tow, and Stephen snapped at her. "I'm going to call the police. That devil's killed old Thorne." As he strode away I became suddenly aware of overwhelming fatigue and sickness. Everything that had happened that day, the drinks with Betty Urquhart, the interview with Doctor Foster, the discovery of Thorne's body, seemed to rise in my throat. I ran for the lavatory, and got there just in time.

When I came out Uncle Miles was waiting for me, full of concern. He suggested that I should go and lie down, saying that there was nothing like your Thomas Lovell after the kind of thing that had happened to me. He came upstairs with me, fidgeted round while I took off my collar and tie, and muttered something about giving me a drawing to go on my wall for my birthday. A couple of minutes after he had gone out I was asleep.

● ● ● ● ●

He's a Vof, somebody said, and then somebody else, *He's not a Vof, he's a Voffer.* The voices, with no faces attached to them, repeated, *He's a Voffer, Voffer, Voffer.* What did they mean? I turned and twisted, trying to get away from them, and opened my eyes. Stephen was saying, "Christopher, Christopher."

The curtains were not drawn. Outside I could see the velvety dark. I yawned. "What time is it?"

"A quarter to ten. I thought you might like a drink." I saw the glass of lemonade in his hand, and realised that I was thirsty.

It was not like Stephen to be so solicitous, and even as I thanked him I understood the reason. He had not heard how I had got on in London. Now I told him.

He rubbed his hands. "Coming down tomorrow. By tomorrow night we'll have him behind bars. But that's not the only reason why I came up. The police are here and they'd like to see you. That is, if you're feeling up to it."

"I'm all right." In fact, as I jumped out of bed and washed my face I felt extremely well and alert.

"You never told me Betty Urquhart had been Uncle Miles' wife."

He tossed his head in an almost girlish way. "Didn't I?"

"I think you might have told me."

"Oh well, I'm sorry."

When I got down into the drawing-room I saw that Lady W had taken charge. She looked ill, her face yellow as a digestive biscuit and her eyes cloudy with pain, but she sat bolt upright in her own particular chair, and everybody else in the room seemed cowed by the mantle of authority that she had resumed. It might be Stephen who had telephoned the police, but it was Mamma who would deal with them. At my entrance she tapped the floor with a malacca stick beside the chair, a little like a conductor calling for attention.

"Christopher. This is Inspector Arbuthnot. He seems to think it necessary that he should question you. I said that I could not object if you were sufficiently recovered."

I said that I had. I don't know what the inspector would have done if I had said anything else. He was a large man, large but not fat, and everything about him was grey. He had grey curly hair, a greyish face, a grey suit, a grey tie and grey socks. I should like to add that he wore a grey shirt and grey shoes, but that would not be true. He listened to Lady W with no sign of impatience, and when I spoke gave me an encouraging nod. With him was Sergeant Hasty, whom I knew. He smiled sheepishly.

"Do you want to talk to him alone? Very well, you may use the morning-room." She said it as if she were making a large concession to this member of the lower orders who by some unlucky chance had moved within her ken. "You will bear in mind that it is really very late."

"I will, Lady Wainwright."

"Anything else can be left until the morning, I hope."

"I should like to talk to other members of the household," the inspector said stolidly.

"Do you wish to talk to me? I have not seen Thorne today. If you wish to see me it must be in my room. I am going to bed."

"I shan't need to worry you tonight, Lady Wainwright."

"Poor Thorne. He would be unhappy to know that he is causing so much trouble." It was an epitaph. She rose. Stephen moved towards her, but she took David's arm. There was silence until they had gone. Then Markle was on his feet.

"Look here, Inspector, I told you that I'm Mr David Wainwright's solicitor. I came down with him because he thought there might be legal problems I could help with, but everything seems to be quite straightforward—"

There was a protesting murmur from Stephen, but it was the inspector who spoke. "Somebody in this household has been murdered. Do you call that quite straightforward?"

Markle spread out his hands. "That's nothing to do with me."

"I still have some questions, Mr Markle."

"Then can't you ask them now? I want to get back to London tonight."

"I am afraid that may not be possible."

"I don't see why not." There was anger in Markle's voice. Then David came back and said quietly that he would like Markle to stay overnight. The solicitor subsided, grumbling.

The morning-room faced north and east and was a cold inhospitable kind of room with a lot of lumpy Victorian furniture in it. The inspector bestowed his bulk in a ladder-back chair and listened while I told him about finding Thorne's body. He didn't make any comment when I told him why I had moved it. Then he said, "You haven't lived here very long, have you?"

"Six years."

"Yes. You hadn't met Mr David Wainwright before his present visit, then. That is, the gentleman who says he is Mr David Wainwright." He was watching me carefully.

"No."

"What do you think about him?"

"I don't see that's of any importance."

"Oh, but it is," he said in his quiet voice that had just a hint of country accent in it. "I gather there's a difference of opinion about whether or not it's Mr Wainwright. But then they may all be a bit, prejudiced, shall I say? For that matter I knew Mr David Wainwright myself, and I don't know whether this is the same man. But your opinion would be, what shall I say, a fresh one, unbiased."

"What has this got to do with Thorne?"

"Nothing perhaps. And then again, perhaps a good deal. Thorne was one of the people who recognised Mr Wainwright, wasn't he? Supposing he'd seen something that made him change his mind, d'you see what I'm getting at? That's why I'd like your opinion, d'you see?"

I said stiffly, "Lady Wainwright's been very kind to me."

He sighed, took out a pipe, looked at it and put it back. "I'm a patient man, but don't try my patience too far, son. I hate coming to houses like this one, you know that? Houses where people think they're better than their neighbours, and what's worse the neighbours think so too. Houses where they let you in on sufferance and shut you away when you want to talk to people, as though you were a bad smell. I'll tell you something. I came here once before, when I was a sergeant, and I was smoking my pipe and I've never forgotten the way Lady Wainwright told me to put it out. Not asked, mind you, told. So just don't tell me how kind she's been to you, son, but answer my question."

All this was said in a voice that impressed me by its very lack of passion. I had not realised before today that people could seriously dislike Lady W, as both Betty Urquhart and now apparently this policeman did. I saw Hasty, who was more my idea of a policeman, one who had a drink or a cup of coffee when he came in, shift uneasily.

"I can't make up my mind," I said. "I accepted him at first, but there have been one or two things that—well, I suppose they're nothing really. Tomorrow, though, two people are coming down—"

As soon as I had spoken the words I knew they were a mistake. "What things?" he said. "And what people?"

I told him about David's reaction when I mentioned his assumed name, and then about Betty Urquhart and Doctor Foster. This seemed to interest him, and he asked whether David knew anything of it.

"I certainly haven't told him."

"And I'll be obliged if you'd say nothing. It may be interesting."

He seemed to have nothing more to say, but I couldn't quite let it go at that. I suppose that what Wilkie Collins calls the detective fever was working in my veins and had been doing so, although without my knowing it, ever since the two men had stepped out of the little beetle car in front of the house. Now that the shock of discovering Thorne's body had faded, I was curious.

"He'd been shot, hadn't he?"

He looked at me as though doubting whether he should answer. "Hit on the head and then shot, yes."

"You haven't—found the weapon?" In my hazy recollection of the few detective stories I had read, police were always finding the weapon.

"Weapons," he amended. "We have not."

"I don't see why you're so sure it's to do with Uncle David coming back."

"Coincidence," Sergeant Hasty said, speaking for the first time. "The guv'nor doesn't like coincidences."

The inspector nodded. "One day the long-lost son comes home, next day this old man is murdered, d'you see? That's a bit too steep."

"But why?"

"I shan't find that out talking to you, shall I? Or talking to the rest of 'em, I dare say. I had enough of that ten years ago. I wouldn't mind if I never saw any of them again."

"What were you investigating ten years ago?"

"A crime. Murder."

Chapter Seven
The Paper in the Ottic

There comes a point in the telling of any first person story, as it seems to me, when the narrator has either to confess himself stumped or to practise some sort of evasion. An example of confessing yourself stumped comes in *The Moonstone*, when the narration changes from the first person narrative of Franklin Blake to that of the steward Gabriel Betteredge, and then on to other people. The objection to this is not merely that Gabriel Betteredge is an old bore, but also that we never really believe that he would be capable of putting pen to paper. Evasion occurs in *Treasure Island*, where the story changes suddenly from Jim Hawkins' narrative to a third person account of things Jim didn't see, although they are described very much as though he *did* see them. Do I hear you saying that I am making too much fuss about something that readers are quite happy to accept as a convention? I don't agree. It would be wrong, as I see it, for me to start describing the inspector's interviews with the other people in the house as though I had been present, lively as I'm sure some of them were. I intend to be fairly strict about it, and to tell you only what I saw and heard myself. I had little to do with the official police investigation, and anyway this isn't an ordinary crime story so much as—I don't know what to call it—a romantic mystery, perhaps.

Sergeant Hasty came out with me, and took Markle away. I wondered whether the inspector was seeing him next to annoy the Wainwrights, or whether he really had some special reason. The rest of them were in the drawing-room. Stephen was grumbling both about the inefficiency of the police and about their discourtesy in making inquiries so late at night, rather as though he had not called them in himself. At the other end of the room David was busy with the whisky bottle. He looked ill, and his hand was shaking. He said what I had been thinking. "You called them in, Brother Stephen."

"Did you hope that they wouldn't be called in?" And he added, "Don't call me Brother Stephen."

"It's your name." David came over and faced me. I realised that he was a little drunk. "What did he say to you?"

"Asked a lot of questions."

"You surprise me. About me?"

I was saved from answering by Clarissa, who barked, "For a man who's seen as much death as you say you have, you're very nervous."

"It doesn't mean you get used to it. Quite the contrary."

Markle was not gone long, and when he returned there was an interchange between him and David. "I'm going back to London," the solicitor said.

"No." David's face twitched. "I need you here. Please."

"Nothing I can do here that I can't do in London." Markle looked round at us with his somehow insulting gaze. "No need to wash our dirty linen here, let's go outside. All right?" he said to Hasty, who nodded. They were outside for five minutes, and I could hear the murmur of voices. Then Markle poked his head inside the door. "Goodbye all. Hope I haven't put you to too much trouble. Be seeing you again, I expect." His head was withdrawn, and we heard his car starting up.

Miles was sitting hunched in a corner. "Thank goodness he's gone. A most objectionable fellow."

"He's a shyster solicitor." Stephen felt at his collar. "I asked a friend of mine about him today, and that's what he told me. The sort of man who goes round after people who've been injured in accidents and offers to make a claim if he gets half the proceeds."

"Good God, are there people like that?" Clarissa bayed.

Stephen looked at me. "You're safe in telling us, now that they've gone. What did the inspector ask you about?"

He used a wheedling tone that didn't suit him. I should find it hard to say what tone did suit Stephen, but he never rubbed me the wrong way so much as when he was trying to be nice. "He asked me about—" I nodded after the departed David, and Stephen nodded too, well pleased. "And he said he'd come here ten years ago on a case."

Silence. Then Stephen said, "That man Arbuthnot is a trouble maker. It takes Mamma to deal with him, she doesn't stand any nonsense."

"I wondered what it was all about. You weren't here?" I said to Uncle Miles, who started.

"No, no. I was with an ENSA party up at Catterick—the camp, you know. But I believe it was a very disagreeable business."

"He said it was murder."

"It had nothing to do with this," Stephen said. "And there's no need to talk about it."

We were silent then, until Hasty reappeared and asked for Uncle Miles. David didn't come back. He had evidently gone to bed, and after vainly trying to get Stephen and Clarissa to talk I followed him. It was nearly midnight. I got into bed and fell asleep immediately, undisturbed by Vofs or Voffers.

● ● ● ● ●

Again I was struck by the different face life wears on a fine morning. Night is the time for extremists, for revolutionaries, illicit loves of all kinds, heavy gamblers, murderers, thieves. Last night I had found it easy to contemplate David as a murderer, and to accept the idea that he might be behind bars by this evening. But in the morning it was much more difficult to believe that this pale worn man in his shabby suit had killed old Thorne. I couldn't really believe, when I came down and found him eating haddock, that I was sitting at breakfast with a murderer.

After breakfast I was walking through the hall when I heard Uncle Miles saying "murderer," and paused to listen. Was it an accusation? What followed undeceived me. In a hoarse whisper the voice went on: "Ten shillings double Lovely Relations in the four-thirty and High Flyer in the five o'clock. That's all, yes." There was the sound of the telephone receiver being replaced, and then Uncle Miles came out of the telephone extension in the hall. He smiled sheepishly. "Just having a little flutter. Life must go on, you know, life must go on."

"Uncle Miles, do you really believe David killed Thorne? I know you say he's not David, but I have to call him something," I added hurriedly.

"Just don't know, my boy, the whole thing's too much for my addled old brain. I can tell you one thing, though. That inspector's got a very hectoring manner. And I'm not talking about Troy."

The world was not wholly changed, I reflected, if Uncle Miles could still make puns.

A few minutes later I found David himself in one of the corridors, looking in an abstracted way through one of the piles of junk that, as I have said already, had accumulated like snowballs in various parts of the house. I asked if there was anything he wanted. He started when I spoke to him, and seemed certainly to have lost the composure of twenty-four hours earlier.

"No, no, I'm just passing the time. Tremendous lot of stuff here, Mamma ought to get rid of it."

"She has got rid of some. All those eighteenth-century military prints that used to be piled up outside your room."

He frowned. "I don't remember them."

"There was a set about Marlborough's campaigns, Blenheim and Malplaquet and so on. General Wainwright liked them, I believe."

He said more decisively, "I don't remember," and this was not surprising because I had just invented the prints. I tried another tack.

"I've been helping with the research on the book. Perhaps we shall be able to get on with that when you're free."

He had been kneeling to look at the things. Now he sat back on his heels and smiled at me, and there was something charming about his smile, "I've got a feeling you're testing me out. Yes, I do know what you're talking about, but I can't say the prospect of delving again into the details of Tel-el-Kebir really stirs me. After the last few years I've had enough of playing soldiers. Besides—"

He had paused. "Besides what?"

"Doctor McNulty came again this morning. He said Mamma can't last more than a week or two, less perhaps.

You knew, didn't you?"

"Yes, I knew." It was true that I knew she could not live long, yet to be faced with the idea of her death as something real and imminent shocked me. Behind my eyes I felt the unfamiliar prick of tears, and I was glad when he turned away, saying soberly, "I'm glad I came back when I did."

I left him, thinking not of the mystery of his identity, but of the reality of death. I had known Lady W for only six years, yet she seemed to have been part of my life for ever. I had a sense, much stronger than the bewilderment I had known at the death of my parents, that the fabric of my life was being torn apart, and that what was happening at Belting would change the pattern of things for ever. I went up to my Thomas Lovell and wandered around the room, touching the Japanese grass paper, looking at the pictures, trying to induce the sense of pleasure that these things had so often given me in the past. This morning they failed, or rather, it was as though I were anaesthetised and could not feel them. I went to the cupboard where I kept the poems and stories I wrote, but never sent to editors. Work, I knew, could be a solace, and there was a fantastic tale called *The Unburied Dead*, which I had started during my last holidays and which I thought I might look at again. But I could not find the story, and it occurred to me that I had probably left it lying about somewhere in the room and that Lily or Jane or Susan or one of our other occasional dailies had put it in the ottic.

The ottic was one of Uncle Miles' whimsical inventions, evolved after I had had a row with Clarissa which had begun absurdly, as so many rows do, by my saying that bull terriers were extremely ugly. After it was over, Uncle Miles said I looked awfully neurotic. He added solemnly:

"When you feel neurotic
Take refuge in the ottic."

I had often done so since then, and in fact one of the ottics had been made into a sort of workroom for me. It was a big room with a covered ceiling and a dormer window, and I would sit up there when I wanted leisure to write or think. A large scrubbed deal table had been put there, and this was often littered with manuscripts, books and pamphlets I was reading, and quill pens, for which at this time I had a passion. Lady W felt a deep admiration for writers of all sorts, and our dailies were given instructions that if they ever found any manuscripts of mine they were to be preserved and put into the ottic.

I could not find *The Unburied Dead* (I may add parenthetically that I discovered later that Uncle Miles had found it in my Thomas Lovell, taken it away to read and left it in the bathroom cupboard—and a wretched piece of writing it was too). I began to look elsewhere. Like so much of the house the ottics were repositories for old trunks, bits of broken furniture, dusty children's games, boxes containing used tennis balls, and so on. It was while I was searching through one of the trunks, that I came across a pile of papers beneath it, and started looking at them. Among the bills from the electricity board and the butcher I found an issue of our local newspaper, the *Kent Record*. I was about to put it aside when I saw that the date was 18th July, 1944, and that a story in it was ringed in black pencil. The story was headed Mysterious Death of Estate Agent. "Was it Foul Play?" asks Coroner.

I sat in an old chair that had been in the ottic as long as I could remember—when I first sat in it I was afraid that rats lurked somewhere in the decayed horsehair with which it was stuffed—and read. I soon realised that Inspector Arbuthnot's reference to coming up here ten years ago on a case must refer to the paper I was reading. The report, for those wartime days, was a long one.

On Wednesday of this week the inquest was held on Edward Charles Sullivan, age 38, of 82 Rampiter Gardens, Folkestone, partner in a firm of local estate agents, who disappeared from his home on 3rd June. Sullivan's body was found in the Grand Military Canal, near Hythe, a fortnight after his disappearance. He had been drowned.

Det. Inspector Greensword gave evidence of the body being discovered by a local girl, and said the cause was asphyxiation from drowning. The Coroner (Mr F Eustace) asked him: "Can you give us any further help? Can you say positively whether or not there was foul play?"

Inspector Greensword: "I cannot do that."

"I understand that the deceased was able to swim, so that if he had fallen into the canal he should have been able to save himself."

"Probably, sir. It would depend on the spot. In any case, the medical evidence is not conclusive."

"I understand that Sullivan had taken a considerable amount of alcohol. How would that affect him?"

"He had taken the equivalent of six pints of beer. The effect would be to slow down his reactions and lessen his resistance. He also had a heart condition, although it was not serious."

Evidence was given by Det.-Sergt. Arbuthnot of finding marks on the towpath near West Hythe on the morning after Sullivan's disappearance, indicating

*that a struggle had taken place. Sullivan was known
to have been in the Duck and Drake nearby, until
closing time. He was alone. C Payne and J Fry, farm
workers, gave evidence that they had heard sounds of
two men quarrelling by the canal, although they could
not recognise voices. Miss Margaret Clay, of Freelands,
near Folkestone, gave evidence that she was engaged to
be married to the deceased, who was in business as an
estate agent with Mr Hugh Wainwright, of Belting. She
had also met Flt.-Lieut. David Wainwright, brother of
the above, and had gone out with him. Sullivan had
objected to this and there had been a quarrel. Sullivan
was of a very jealous disposition. She knew Sullivan
and Flt.-Lieut. Wainwright had had an argument, but
did not know any details. On the night of 3rd June she
attended a "Victory War Fund" meeting, and after that
went straight home.*

*Flt.-Lieut. Wainwright said that he knew Sullivan,
and also knew Miss Clay. He was on leave, and had
seen her once or twice.*

*The Coroner: "Were you carrying on an affair with
her?"*

*Flt.-Lieut. Wainwright: "We were friends, nothing
more."*

"But Sullivan objected to the association?"

"Yes, he did."

*"And there were quarrels? Did he on one occasion
tell you to keep away from Miss Clay or there would
be trouble?" The witness agreed that there had been
something like that. He denied that he had said he
would see Miss Clay as often as he liked, and that she
naturally preferred a man in uniform to a civilian.*

He also denied that he had seen Sullivan on the night
of 3rd June. That had been the last night on leave of
his brother, Sergeant Wainwright, and they had spent
it at home. Sergeant Wainwright had gone abroad on
D-Day, and had since been reported missing, believed
killed. Evidence was given by Lady Wainwright, another
brother Mr S Wainwright, and domestics, to the effect
that Flt.-Lieut. Wainwright had spent the evening at
home.

The Coroner said that they might have their suspi-
cions, but suspicion was not proof. They were bound to
ask, "Was it foul play?", but the medical evidence did
not greatly help them. They must not be swayed by gossip.

The jury brought in a verdict that Sullivan had died
of drowning, but that there was not sufficient evidence
to show whether or not this was accidental.

Just before I had finished reading, I became aware that my
name was being called, but my absorption was too great to
permit me to reply. Peterson's head appeared at the door.
Her sergeant-major's eye glared at me.

"Didn't you hear me calling, Mr Christopher? Her ladyship wants you. Important. I've been looking all over for you."

I followed her down the stairs and along to Lady W's
room. Her back was rigid, her face grim. I might have been
a man on a charge led in to the commanding officer, and
it was difficult when following her not to adopt a hands-
in-pocket slouch in reaction. At the door I could not resist
saying, "I can find my way in."

"She's very ill." She glared at me, and turned away.

When I got inside I saw with surprise that they were all
there. Stephen and Clarissa sat very close to each other, he
white and thin, she brick-red and solid so that I was put in

mind of Jack Sprat and his wife. Miles sat picking his nose, which was a bad habit of his when nervous, and David was apart from the others with one leg nonchalantly crossed over the other knee in what I have often been told is the characteristic attitude of an English gentleman, although from my observation this is far from invariably true.

But at first I had no eyes for anybody but Lady W. She was propped up against pillows, and she looked so frail that I had the impression that she had no power to maintain herself, and that if the pillows were removed she would simply sink back in the bed. She had in one hand a small handkerchief with which she kept dabbing at her face as if it were damp, although it looked as dry and brittle as brandysnap. Her voice was thin but clear.

My face must have shown something of what I felt, for she spoke to me. "Christopher. Here at last. Don't look like that, boy, it's that damned doctor. He takes it out of me. I don't know why I pay him to come, the very sight of him makes me feel worse. I wanted to get you all together." The handkerchief patted her face. "I've sent for Humphries."

Somebody exhaled a deep breath. Humphries was the family solicitor.

"David coming back makes a difference. You all understand that, don't you?"

She looked from one face to another, and none of them said anything. It seemed to me inexplicable. I see now that they were all afraid of saying they believed David to be an impostor, because if they did so Lady W might in her present state of mind cut them out of her new will. But although I was subconsciously aware of this, my primary feeling was indignation. Why couldn't they say what they thought. I found myself saying it for them.

"Uncle Miles and Uncle Stephen don't believe he is David." Defiantly I added, "I'm not sure I believe it either."

"And since you never met him your opinion is very much worth having." Her dark eyes blazed at me for a moment, her finger pointed. "Do you think I wouldn't know him?"

"Don't excite yourself, Mamma," Stephen said, and I saw him nudge Clarissa, who got up immediately, lurched towards the bed on her bow legs and gave powerful pats to the pillows. My remark was not followed up. I did not look at Stephen and Miles, I felt so ashamed of them. Lady W went on.

"I wanted you all to know this, I don't want anything hole and corner. There must be changes. But I shan't forget any of my children. I count you as one of them, Christopher." I muttered something. "But you must understand that David coming back makes a difference."

"I should have come before." He turned away from her as he said it, and I was the only one able to see the look of misery on his face.

"Stay with me a little while." She put out her hand to him, and it was a signal for the rest of us to go.

The door had hardly closed behind us when Stephen turned on me. "Why did you say that, what are you trying to do?"

"If you won't say anything—"

"We can speak for ourselves, thank you," Clarissa bayed. "And I can assure you we shall, in our own time."

"Why didn't you say something?" I asked Uncle Miles.

He shook his head at me and scratched his chin. "You're a better man than I am, Gunga Din."

I was hot with anger at the sneakish way they conspired, at the sheer wretched pettiness of them. "Anyway, I've found out a good deal of what you're trying to hide."

Stephen tugged at his collar, and then led the way into the drawing-room. There he said: "Say what you mean."

I told them what I had read in the paper. Stephen said: "If it were David, do you think he would have come back?"

"Because of the case?"

"Because the police knew we were telling lies. And the police knew. Greensword was polite enough, but that man Arbuthnot—"

"You weren't here," I said to Uncle Miles.

"No. I was up in Catterick, entertaining the licentious soldiery."

"I was here," Clarissa said unexpectedly. "There was a great song and dance. Stephen and I were engaged to be married. My father wanted me to break it off."

Stephen gave her a frozen grin that showed his teeth, and I was reminded of what Betty Urquhart had said. "Why don't you get in touch with the dentist who did David's teeth? If he had a record of fillings, that would be as good as a fingerprint, wouldn't it?"

Stephen transferred the grin to me. "Oddly enough that had occurred to us. You aren't the only one with brains here, even if you have won a history scholarship. Our dentist was a man named Faber. He was up in London, not down here. He was killed in a flying bomb raid, and his records were wiped out too."

"Did you know Sullivan?"

"He was always slapping people on the back and making bad jokes. 'You can't do that there 'ere,' have you heard that phrase?" I shook my head. "It was used a great deal in the war by people like Sullivan. He came up here once or twice. He was a partner with Hugh in an estate agents' business."

"And Margaret Clay?"

"Sullivan's girl friend?" That was Clarissa. "I don't know what happened to her, do you, Stephen?"

"I think there's more to be found out about Sullivan," I said. "I shan't be in to lunch."

"Where are you going?"

"Folkestone." I went up to the ottic, picked up the *Kent Record* and dashed down the stairs. On the way I passed David, coming along the corridor from Lady W's room. He looked like a man released from prison.

Chapter Eight

Lunch with Mr Ulfheim

At this time I had never been out of England, though I had a passport obtained three years earlier when Uncle Miles had proposed that we should go together on a skiing holiday in Austria, a project which had to be abandoned when he broke his leg while practising on the slopes of an indoor skiing school. I had never gone on a summer holiday as such, for Lady W regarded life at Belting as holiday enough for anybody. In those days Folkestone seemed to me a fascinating place, and I still regard it as the second best of the south coast seaside resorts. The best is Brighton, and if Dr Johnson were alive today no doubt he would say that a man who is tired of Brighton is tired of life, for Brighton contains all that London has to offer and gives as a bonus the pleasures of the sea and of those fingers sticking into it, the piers.

But to come back to Folkestone. I loved the little zig-zag paths that went down to the lower level from which one might approach the sea, the water-drawn lift cage in which for twopence (it costs more now) one might go down or of course up, for the cars work in couples, to the deliciously ugly red brick Victorian lifthouse, the small shops around the harbour and the harbour itself, the rows of solid hotels that stand back from the front, with their formidable promise of Edwardian meals, big bedrooms with gigantic wardrobes in them, battles for the bathroom. I should add that my vision of the hotels was imaginary, for I had not been inside any of them, and have never visited them yet.

When I went along to the *Kent Record* office it was shut, so I went back to the front, walked down the zig-zag and along to the small fun fair that opens during the summer. Here I rode on the dodgems, and went in a thing called the "Loop-de-Loop" which made me feel slightly sick. The sickness passed away when I ate some candy floss, and I strolled round looking at the side shows. Professor Bump the phrenologist, who had once read my bumps and predicted, after a few shrewd preliminary questions, that I should be either a famous writer or a professional cricketer, was talking to Peter Portland, who ran the Kwik Fire Fotographic Service.

"Just ups and offs without so much as a by your leave," Peter said. "I mean, it just isn't right."

"It's not professional conduct," the Professor agreed, picking his teeth gloomily.

I knew them both, and asked what they were talking about. The Professor indicated the stall that stood between them. It said in large letters MONSIEUR MAGIQUE, and in smaller ones: "Fresh From France. Konjuring for the Kiddies. See the Great Disappearing Act and say Oh la la with Monsieur Magique."

"What's wrong then?"

"What's wrong? Just that he's *cleared off*, that's all," Peter said indignantly. "Engaged for three weeks, and then says he's not doing *enough business*."

"And he's packing 'em in, mind you, packing 'em in." That was the Professor. "Especially the kiddies."

"I don't see why it matters to you."

It was a rash remark. Peter puffed out his cheeks. "Do you think that we want a blank space between us, something that's *closed down*? It's bad, it puts people off."

The Professor threw away his tooth-pick. "I'm writing to the Entertainments Department at the Town 'All. They can get someone else 'ere, someone from this side of the Channel too, thank you."

I left them bemoaning the low ethical standards prevailing in their profession, and took the water lift back to the top. This time the office, which was just off the High Street, was open. When I gave my name and asked whether I could look at the file for 1944 I was taken past the flap barrier of the counter into a small office which contained a desk, a typewriter, and a great many papers and files. The girl behind the desk took off her horn-rimmed spectacles to look at me, and then put them on again.

"If you like to clear some of the junk off that chair you can sit down." I did so. "And what can we do for you, Mr Barrington?"

I told her what I wanted, and she levelled on me a long appraising gaze. Then she said, "The file for 1944 is on the second shelf above your head. Help yourself."

The file was bulky, and it was dusty. When I asked her for a duster she looked at me as though I were mad, and then spoke to the boy outside, who produced some kind of rag. I dusted off the file, found June, 1944, and the issue that recorded Sullivan's disappearance, and went on from there. I don't know what I had expected, but the result was sparse. There were a few lines about the disappearance ("Estate Agent Vanishes"), then next week a statement that the police were following up clues and that Sullivan was believed to have had a quarrel on the night of his disappearance, then the issue I had seen, and then stories in the following two weeks, one saying that the dead man's brother George Sullivan was not satisfied with the verdict, and the next saying that the firm of Sullivan and Wainwright was closing down. And that seemed to be all. I closed the file.

"Did you find what you wanted?" It was the girl again, looking at me with a direct gaze from dark blue eyes. "What *do* you want exactly, Mr Barrington?"

I saw no reason to beat about the bush. "I'm trying to find out something about an old murder case. It was in 1944, and—"

She took off the glasses. "I thought you were. Shouldn't you ask me, then? I'm Elaine Sullivan."

"You're not his daughter?"

"Ted Sullivan wasn't married." Of course I had known that. "I'm George Sullivan's daughter."

"You know all about it, then."

"I doubt if anyone knows all about it, not even the police. But I know something. I know who you are, too."

"You do?"

"A cousin of mine is at school with you," she said, and I remembered the Sullivan who was a member of the Æsthetes' Group. Had he once said he had relatives in Folkestone? I believed he had. But she had not stopped talking. "And anyway the Sullivans know all about the Wainwrights, or they used to. Since my father died a couple of years ago and my sister got married and went to live in Stoke, there's nobody to take an interest. I know about your murder too, the odd-job man, isn't it? And someone said David Wainwright had come back, is that right?" I hesitated. "You're like the rest of them."

"How do you mean?"

In savage mockery she said, "This is one of the lower orders, can I trust her with the secrets of the gentry, would it be proper? Though *you're* not the gentry, from what I hear."

"No, I'm not." Perhaps I coloured, I don't know. "I'm a poor relation, if that's the way you want to put it. I don't see why you've got such a chip on your shoulder about it."

"A chip on my shoulder." She stared at me through the horn-rims. "I hate the bloody Wainwrights. That ghastly old snob and her horrible sons, I hate them all."

It had become clear to me in the last couple of days that my view of the Wainwright family was not shared by most of the other people who knew them. The fact that this discovery had come to me as a shock shows how sharply the imagination is limited by the physical world surrounding it. At Belting Lady W's word was law, servants were respectful, there was nobody to contradict Stephen when he deplored the state of the country or Clarissa when she lamented the impossibility of getting a decent kennel maid. I had accepted all this, and in my ignorance had assumed that everybody else would accept it too. I was amazed to hear Lady W called a snob, just as I had been astounded when Betty Urquhart said she devoured her family. I dare say the shocks were salutary, but they were far from pleasant.

In a milder tone she said, "The Sullivans have got no reason to love the Wainwrights. Those precious brothers wrecked Ted's life between them, and my father's too."

"Which brothers?"

"Hugh and David." She took the glasses off, put them on the table in front of her. "Hugh ruined Ted, David killed him, and then the family got my father sacked from his job."

I gaped at her. "I don't believe it."

"Do you want to hear about it, or is the Wainwright

feeling too strong for you to listen?" What could I do but listen, when she said that? "Let's begin with Uncle Ted. He was a commercial traveller, sold men's clothing, not doing too badly for himself by any means, when he met Hugh and David Wainwright at Folkestone races. I remember he came back full of it—he was single, and he lodged with us when he wasn't on the road—saying how decent they were, not a bit toffee-nosed as you might expect. Then he took them to a few betting clubs he knew, and so on, and a couple of weeks later he brought them back home to supper, and told us about this idea they had of starting a business together. But do you know what happened before that? He'd lent Hugh Wainwright two hundred pounds to settle some debt of his brother's."

So that was where the money had come from. "Did he get it back?"

"In a way," she said reluctantly. "Hugh was supposed to put two hundred extra into the business. But before we get on to that I'd like to make you see things the way they were, though I don't know if I can. My father worked as a garage mechanic, this was before the war, you understand, and he thought himself lucky to have a job. There was nothing wrong with the house we lived in, it was clean and decent and it even had a bathroom, but it was a working-class house, you understand what I mean. Uncle Ted had money in the bank, but that two hundred must have made a hole in it. He lent the money just because one of the Wainwrights asked him, are you beginning to understand? And then you've never seen such a hullabaloo as my mother made when she learned they were coming. We ate in the front room instead of the kitchen, she cooked a piece of beef and we usually only had a joint at weekends, and Uncle Ted came in with a dozen bottles of beer. I was only a kid at the time, of course, and I said to my mother 'It's like Christmas.' I can tell you I was excited. And then they came."

"Hugh and David?"

"That's right. I stayed up to supper and saw them." Reluctantly again, she said, "They were very nice. Mother said afterwards 'I must say they've got no side about them,—it's as though they were like ourselves,' and Uncle Ted—said, 'What did I tell you, they're real gentlemen, we're going to make a fortune.' Only my father was against it and how right he was."

"What were they like, Hugh and David?" I had very strongly now the sense that I had learned only partial truths about them, that there was something more to be found out, and that this something more might be important.

"They didn't look alike, Hugh was dark and David fair, and David was very handsome. Hugh was the talker, he was always talking and laughing as if everything was a tremendous joke, and David was different, he had a very gentle face, still looked like a boy. Mother said afterwards that he looked so shy and delicate it was natural for any woman to want to look after him." She said fiercely, "She didn't know then that he was going to kill Uncle Ted."

"Tell me about that."

"Well, they started this business, Uncle Ted and Hugh. Uncle Ted and father both put all their savings into it— Father only did it because Uncle Ted made such a song and dance—and Hugh put up money too, I suppose it came from his mother, and it was supposed to include the money he owed Uncle Ted. The firm was called Wainwright and Sullivan, estate agents, and the idea was that with Uncle Ted's connections and the prestige of the Wainwright name, they couldn't lose. But not long after they got properly started the war came, and the bottom dropped out of the house market, and then Hugh went into the army and Uncle Ted had to run the firm on his own. Then he met Margaret Clay."

"What was she like?"

"If you ask me she was just a tart. No, that's wrong." She played with the glasses on the desk, put them on again. "She was out for a good time, I suppose, like a lot of girls during the war, and she took in Uncle Ted, because he thought she was different. In a way he was like what you'd expect a commercial traveller to be, full of jokes and catch phrases, but in other ways he was—innocent, I suppose you'd call it. He volunteered for service when the war began, but he had something wrong with his heart and they wouldn't take him. Afterwards he used to go round saying, 'Don't you know there's a war on?' Do you remember people saying that?" I shook my head. "Or he'd say, 'Yes, we have no bananas,' or when things were going wrong he would say, 'We must just soldier on,' and march round the room as though a band were playing. Oh, I can see that Wainwright look on your face, but there was nothing wrong with Uncle Ted, I loved him. Nothing wrong, except that he trusted the Wainwrights. And that he fell for Margaret Clay. I was listening behind the door when he told my father he was going to marry her, and my father—he was working in a factory, not called up—told him not to be a bloody fool. But he got engaged, just the same. That was in 1944, just before Hugh and David both came home on leave."

"And then?"

"I didn't see either of them, but one night Hugh came to the house when my parents were out, and I heard him having a terrific row with Uncle Ted. That must have been over David. And another night there was a real show-down, Margaret came back with Uncle Ted and David, and the three of them had it out together. I heard her say she wasn't married yet, and she'd go out with anyone she liked. Uncle Ted said he'd do for David if he found him with her again. Afterwards my father said to my mother, 'What d'you expect from a Wainwright but lying and cheating?' That was a couple of days before Uncle Ted was killed."

"What about the night he died?"

She shook her head. "I don't know anything about that, except what my father always said. That they lied themselves silly in the witness box. He said the police thought so too. Hugh had been posted missing by then, but Lady Wainwright and Stephen and David went into the witness box and swore they'd all spent the evening in the house, David had never gone out. They don't mind lying when it's a matter of saving their skins."

"What do you think happened?"

"David went out and met Uncle Ted, they had another row, and he killed him. That's what happened." She looked at the clock and said abruptly, "I shouldn't say no if you asked me to lunch."

I had only six or seven shillings in my pocket. It is the kind of situation that embarrasses the young. "I'm terribly sorry, I'm afraid I—"

She laughed. "Is it that bad? I thought all Wainwrights, even adopted ones, had wads of cash in their wallets. Let's have lunch on the *Record*, then. I'll take it out of the till and old Stingy will have to like it. After all, I'm interviewing you in connection with a local murder."

"Who's old Stingy?"

"The editor."

"Is he here?"

"No, this is just a branch office. One girl, a boy, and part-time photographer. I'm the girl, and I'm in charge. Didn't you know local newspapers run on a shoestring? Coming?" She looked at the glasses, then snapped them decisively into a case.

"Why do you keep putting them on and taking them off?"

"I'm only twenty. Too young. Nothing wrong with my eyes, but people take you more seriously if you wear glasses. No kidding, that's true."

Even today Folkestone is not conspicuous for good eating places, and years ago that was much truer than it is now. Elaine Sullivan led the way, briskly and purposefully, into the old part of the town, and suddenly dived down some steps. While we walked along I was able to observe that she had a stocky figure, with sturdy peasant legs. Her face was dark and strong, fierce-browed and full-lipped. I found her attractive.

We were in a small room, decorated with Chinese lanterns, and with Chinese waiters. "Best place to eat in Folkestone," she said. "Hope you like Chinese food, if not you'll just have to pretend."

I did not like to tell her that I had never eaten it before, nor to mention my Japanese bedroom in case she thought I was boasting of it in a Wainwright manner. I let her order, and only demurred at eating with chopsticks. We drank a sort of seaweed soup, watery but pleasant. I said some of the things that had occurred to me as we walked from the office to the restaurant.

"I know what my next step is." She raised her thick brows. "I shall talk to Margaret Clay."

"You'll have to go to New Zealand. She married an engineer after the war, and went out there. And you realise my father talked to her at the time. Why should she say things to you that she wouldn't say to him?"

I had no answer, and returned to something she had said in the office. "You said your father lost his job. How did that happen?"

She spooned her soup. "With Ted and Hugh both dead, of course the firm couldn't be carried on. Lady Wainwright swooped down with an accountant, and he discovered that there was practically no money left. This came as a bit of a shock to everybody, and my father really couldn't understand it, but anyway she was quite good about it. And it turned out, by the way, that she knew about the two hundred pounds borrowed from Uncle Ted, she'd given that as part of the capital for the business. However, she paid my father back all the money he'd lost, and I suppose you could say that was generous."

"I should certainly think so."

"But my father was one of the awkward squad, and he got it into his head that she was bribing him to keep quiet about Uncle Ted's death. When the war was over he kept pestering the police to start up inquiries again, and then tried to start them himself. Within a few weeks the owner of the firm he was working for then called him in and sacked him, saying he wasn't doing his job properly."

"Perhaps he wasn't."

She glared. "He was a good mechanic, and they were in short supply. The owner was a man named Gibson. He was a friend of Lady Wainwright."

"Excuse me. I couldn't help overhearing your conversation. I wonder whether I might be of assistance."

A man was standing beside our table. He was plump rather than tall, a round-faced smiling man of about forty, dressed in neat dark clothes. "You were talking about the tragedy that took place ten years ago, and it is a subject in which I am personally interested. You see, I was there."

"Where?" Elaine asked aggressively.

"Where else but at the Duck and Drake, on the fatal evening."

"And who are you?"

"My name is Ulfheim." He smiled broadly, with a gleam of gold teeth.

"You didn't give evidence at the inquest."

"Indeed I didn't." By now Mr Ulfheim had drawn up a chair and was sitting down. "You don't mind if I join you? The more who share the feast the greater the store of wisdom at their command, is I believe an old Confucian saying." He leaned over and transferred a large shabby suitcase from the next table. "But in reply to your question, I had good reasons for absenting myself from the inquest."

"What sort of reasons?" I asked.

"A difficult question. I am, what shall I say, a traveller. A traveller in clerical vestments masquerading under the name of the Reverend Strawman. You don't believe me?" He opened the suitcase and drew from it what did certainly seem to be some sort of black cassock-like robe. There was something clerical, too, or the caricature of something clerical, about the plumpness of his cheeks and the whiteness of his hands. Below the robe I glimpsed briefly a number of wooden objects, with thin wires or loops attached to them. Then, with a sly look at me, he closed the case again. "I can see that you don't believe me, you think I am telling you a traveller's tale. Shall I say then that I have a splendid line in pornographic postcards which I sell under the pretence of being a traveller in clerical vestments? But here come our dishes. What a great deal of food." He began to help himself with zest.

Elaine put on her spectacles. The effect intimidated me, but appeared to afford only amusement to Mr Ulfheim. "If you've got anything to tell us, I suggest you tell it."

"All in good time, Miss Sullivan. It is Miss Sullivan, isn't it? Sweet and sour pork, my favourite. Of course you are lunching with Ulfheim, that is understood. And Mr Christopher Barrington, I presume. Stirring times at Belting, aren't they, Mr Barrington? What do they make of the return of the native?"

"If you mean David Wainwright, his brothers don't believe it is David."

"Don't they, now? What about his mother, is she a sceptic too?"

"No. She says it is David."

"Well, well, a house divided. That's distressing." Mr Ulfheim was adept with his chopsticks, darting about here and there among pork and chicken and noodles while he glanced quickly from me to Elaine and back again. "And Thorne's death, that's distressed everybody too, I expect."

"It's obvious that the police think David did it."

"He's worried, eh, would you say he was worried? I can see you would. Poor David. If it is David."

Adept though Mr Ulfheim was with the chopsticks—and Elaine was not far behind him—I outpaced them with my fork and spoon. I put them down now. "Mr Ulfheim, the idea was that you were going to tell us something, do you remember? Not that you should pump us. You haven't told us anything yet, not even how you know our names."

"Ah, you've seen through my little stratagem. Never trust a traveller in clerical vestments, who calls himself Strawman, that's a motto of antique wisdom. Especially when he tells you that his real name is Ulfheim. You'd guessed that wasn't the truth, I expect. Yes, I see you had. You will have to accept that I know your names when you haven't had the pleasure of knowing mine, but I really have got something to tell you." He paused, and said with dramatic emphasis, "Miss Sullivan, your uncle was not killed by David Wainwright."

"You mean he was killed by somebody else?" Elaine said sharply.

"You catch my drift. And who was the somebody else? That's the question, or so you may think. But you would be wrong. The question is, why was Ted Sullivan killed? And I can give you the answer to it. He was killed because he knew too much about a certain group of people who were very active here at that time."

"What sort of people?" I asked.

"People, shall I say, who were not anxious that we should win the war."

"Do you mean pro-Germans? Here, in Kent?" Elaine asked incredulously.

"And what is so surprising about that, my dear young lady? What do you know about life during the war? The question is rhetorical, for it is plain that you are not of an age to know anything at all."

"I can read."

"I don't dispute it. Have you heard of the Link?"

"It was a sort of pro-German organisation, isn't that right? But I thought it was really quite respectable."

"And so it was, my dear, so it was. Respectable gentlemen were members of it, MPs and retired admirals, entirely inno-cent people who in some cases suffered for being credulous about Hitler's Germany. But these people were used by the real agents. Folkestone is on the coast, you can imagine the importance of that. There was a Link group here, and some members of it were interned for the duration. But behind the Link in Kent there were other people, and they were not interned." He scooped up the last grains of rice, the last piece of pork. "Your uncle stumbled across them, Miss Sullivan. That's why he died."

We both sat looking at him. "Why are you telling us this?" I asked.

"Because you are amateurs, my dear young people. You may cause trouble to professionals."

"What professionals?" Elaine said.

"Ulfheim, shall I say? Or Strawman?"

"You want us to give up trying to find out what happened to my uncle?"

For the first time Mr Ulfheim showed signs of irritation. "What happened to your uncle is over and done with. I am concerned about what is likely to happen in the next few days. As for you two, of course you will do what you like, but don't blame me if you run into danger, and don't expect any help." He looked at his watch. "I must go. Thank you for the pleasure of your company. Do you think the police really suspect David Wainwright?"

"I don't see how they can fail to," I replied.

"I must have a word with Arbuthnot." He called for the bill. Elaine and I looked at each other and then she spoke for both of us.

"You can't just leave it at that. You've got to tell us more of what it's all about."

"But indeed I can leave it at that, and I shall." He rose. Something about him suggested a character actor slightly overplaying his part. He seemed about to say something, and then waved a hand—the hand that was not holding his shabby suitcase—and was threading his way among the tables. I was prepared to sit back, sip the tea that had come to us in cups without handles, and discuss him, but Elaine said: "Come on."

"Where?"

"After him. He's not English."

"How do you know?"

"The general look of him. And that tie came from France." Meekly I followed her determined figure as she moved towards the exit. How could she say with such enviable certainty that a tie came from France and not from the Burlington Arcade? Later I learned that this was part of her personality, that dogmatic assertiveness came as naturally to her as atrocious punning did to Uncle Miles. Above ground, we looked to left and right. Then she cried out, "There he is."

Sure enough, Mr Ulfheim was turning a corner into one of the streets that led down to the harbour. We walked after him, turned the corner ourselves, and saw him some thirty yards ahead. He walked quickly, but in a slightly pigeon-toed manner, and I was thinking that we should have no trouble in keeping track of him when he suddenly dashed across the road and disappeared into a narrow side turning. Our reactions were typical. I stopped and said, "How on earth did he know we were following him? He never turned round."

Elaine did not reply but began to run. Again I followed her. As we ran she gasped out, "They have periscopes, things they hold up to see behind them."

We had almost reached the corner when I bumped into a man coming the other way. A well-known voice said, "What do you think you're doing?" and then, with recognition, "What's your hurry, why the flurry?"

I found myself clasped in the arms of Uncle Miles.

Chapter Nine

Scene in a Courtyard

"You almost knocked me over." I was held effectively in Uncle Miles' arms, and even Elaine paused for a few seconds before running to the corner of the alley. She came back. "He's gone."

I attempted explanation. "It was a man, he crossed the road suddenly and ran down there."

Uncle Miles looked at us as if we had taken leave of our senses. "What man? Who was he?"

"He said his name was Ulfheim. Or it might have been Strawman."

"Strawman?" Uncle Miles began to giggle and then the giggle turned into a laugh. He pointed to the name on the corner. It said *Brick Alley*. Between gasps of laughter he asked, "Do you suppose he's a bit of the straw they make bricks out of? He's vanished into the bricks, that's where he's gone. Strawman into Brick Alley."

I began to laugh too. Elaine looked at me in amazement.

"Strawman," I said. "Went into Brick Alley. Can't make bricks without straw, do you get it?"

"Yes. And that's funny?"

I gave up. Uncle Miles coughed. I introduced him and explained, as I felt I had to, that she was the niece of Ted Sullivan.

He looked hunted. "I told you I wasn't at home, I don't know anything about it."

"No Wainwright wants to remember it or know much about it, isn't that right?" Elaine demanded militantly. She had put on her glasses. "It's no good going after that man now, whatever his name was. And anyway, I must get back to the office."

"Shall I see you again?" I was aware that I wanted to.

"You'll find the number in the book."

Uncle Miles gazed after her. "What a forceful young woman. Whatever were you doing together? I don't suppose you'll tell me. But I have a bone to pick with you, Christopher. Let us find somewhere to pick it in peace."

Five minutes later we were settled in the tea lounge of one of Folkestone's stuffier restaurants. While we were talking there, and Uncle Miles was ordering coffee and sweet biscuits, of which he was very fond, I had been trying to solve a problem. Had Mr Ulfheim bolted down Brick Alley because he wanted to avoid Uncle Miles, had Uncle Miles put his arms round me in order effectively to check our pursuit of Mr Ulfheim? Or had Mr Ulfheim simply been engaged in getting away from us? I could not ignore the fact that through meeting Uncle Miles we had lost Mr Ulfheim, yet looking at his red face and bald head, considering his air of pettish annoyance and the way in which it was assuaged by the sweet biscuits, it was hard to associate him with anything that required even a small amount of devious cunning.

"We should have had tea," Uncle Miles said abruptly.

"Why?"

"Because you need tannin." I laughed dutifully. "You didn't tell me you'd been to see that woman."

For a moment I couldn't think what he was talking about. "You mean Betty Urquhart?"

"That terrible woman."

I said mendaciously, "I thought Stephen would have told you."

He bit into another biscuit. "Stephen's conduct was absolutely—" Words failed him, and it was not often that words of a sort failed Uncle Miles. He began again. "He told me late this morning, when it was unavoidable. She is coming down to Belting this afternoon. I said that I should not be there, it was quite impossible for me to meet her. And I told him what I thought of his behaviour. I did not even stay for lunch." That was serious indeed. It was almost unknown for Uncle Miles to be away at lunch-time, unless he was going to a cricket match or a race meeting. "I ate here in Folkestone, very poorly I may say."

"I'm sorry." And I did feel contrite, almost responsible for the poorness of that lunch. "I meant to say something, but didn't know how to. And then everything seemed to happen at once, and I really forgot about it."

"Aren't you going to eat those biscuits?"

"No. Do have them."

His acceptance of them signified the making of peace between us. "What did you think of her? What did she say about me?"

I gave him a carefully edited account of our meeting. Miles sighed, with a note both of regret and of relief. "Marrying her was the greatest mistake of my life."

"Oh, I don't know. I liked her."

"I dare say you did. She was always mad about men. That

was her trouble." He spoke as if it were something chronic, like indigestion. "She seemed to be happy, then?"

"I think so. She's naturally gay, isn't she?"

He looked at me, and pushed away the last biscuit with distaste. "Kent are playing Derbyshire here at Folkestone, did you know that? I shall spend the afternoon there. If you'd like to come—or would it be too much of a fag?" I must explain at this distance of time that Arthur Fagg was then Kent's opening batsman.

"No, I shall go back to Belting. I want to see what happens when Betty and Doctor Foster meet David."

I regretted calling him David as soon as I had spoken, but Uncle Miles didn't notice. "Give her my kind regards." He seemed conscious of the inadequacy of the phrase. "Don't tell her I went away because of her coming, she was always saying that I ran away from things. I suppose you think she's right."

It seemed impossible to answer this. I described Ulfheim and asked Uncle Miles if he had met him.

"No, I don't think so. In fact I'm sure I haven't. I don't know what you're playing at, but don't do anything silly." He smiled with a sort of wistful unhappiness. "That's a silly thing to say, isn't it? I shall do what people always do in their dotage, go and watch the cricket."

• ● ● ● •

The bus got me back to Belting by three o'clock. Neither Betty Urquhart nor Foster had arrived, and in fact there seemed to be nobody about. At least, that was my impression until I found Inspector Arbuthnot in a corner of the drawing-room. In the daylight he looked less grey, but not much less ill-at-ease. He greeted me with what might almost have been called warmth, and asked what I had been doing in Folkestone. I did not want to tell him about Mr Ulfheim, for fear that he would warn me off making any further investigation, and so said that I had been shopping. He asked when the visitors were coming.

"Some time this afternoon, I don't know when. That's why you're here, is it, to see what happens when they meet him?"

"Of course."

"And if they confirm that it is David you'll arrest him? But for which murder?"

He stared at me. "What d'you mean?"

"I've found the details of Ted Sullivan's death. I've talked to his niece, Elaine Sullivan—"

"So that's what you were doing in Folkestone."

"I know you suspected David of killing Sullivan then, but I suppose you hadn't got enough evidence. So if this man had been David he wouldn't have come back, knowing that a murder charge might still be hanging over his head."

He took out his pipe, looked at it, and said, "Damn it, I'm going to smoke my pipe, even if I am in the Wainwright home." When he had lighted it with an air of defiance he went on, "So you think I had David Wainwright marked down for Ted Sullivan, do you? It wasn't my case, you know that, it was Greensword's, and he was a cautious old devil. They lied themselves silly up here, you may have heard that if you've been talking to the Sullivan girl. If it'd been me in charge I'd have put them through the mill, but it's easy to say that when you're just a sergeant and don't have to carry the can. Greensword was cagey, he was thinking of his pension. Let's go in the garden. In here I feel as if I ought to swallow all the smoke."

We walked out into the big courtyard and down by the tennis court. Arbuthnot puffed at his pipe. I noticed that his grey suit was shiny at the elbows. "Supposing I was to tell you that I never suspected David Wainwright of killing Sullivan, would you be surprised?"

"Very surprised. Is that what you are telling me? What about Margaret Clay?"

"Margaret Clay." He dismissed her with a wave of the pipe. "That's not the way things were. I mean, that's not the thing that mattered."

"Then there was nothing to stop David from coming back?"

"As far as we were concerned, nothing. I believe you're holding out on me, young man. You've found out something, or think you have, and you're not passing it on. I'll only say to you, don't do it."

I breathed deeply, took the plunge. "Is it right that Sullivan stumbled across a nest of pro-Germans, and one of them killed him?"

His big head jerked up. "Who told you that?"

I did not feel that I could say. If Ulfheim wanted this passed on to Arbuthnot, he could do it himself. But it seemed to me that I saw what was implied. "This person is still in the district, am I right? And something about David's return made things difficult for him."

He did not reply. A red sports car had entered the drive as that beetle car had done long ago, or in a time that seemed long ago. But where the beetle had come over the cattle grid with decent caution this car clattered across it at thirty miles an hour and swept past us before turning dramatically, with a screech of tyres, into the space before the house. There were two people in it, and one of them was Betty Urquhart. She was the passenger. The man in the driver's seat was a handsome young Negro. As we approached them, Betty saw me and waved. She had a bright-coloured handkerchief round her head which she took off, shaking her bronze curls. She wore a grey jersey and bright scarlet slacks. Her companion had on a thin suit of light coffee colour with a dazzling tie held in place by a clip and black suede shoes that ended in needle points.

The inspector murmured, "Miss Urquhart, I presume. And friend."

I introduced him, and she raised her brows. "Don't tell me the queen bee has called in the police. Oh, by the way, this is Max Miners, he's an action painter. I must say the old pile looks just exactly the same at it did. I'd hoped it might be nearer to falling down. Where *is* everybody? Or are they all dead and buried, as they should be? In particular, where's my ex? I can't wait to see what he looks like. I told you I had an ex living here, didn't I, Max?"

"Sure you told me," Max Miners said. He put a hand on her arm, and I realised that she was distinctly drunk. I understood also, and it was my first lesson in one of the most disconcerting facts of life, how different people look in different surroundings. Seen in her natural ambience Betty Urquhart had delighted me by her forthright naturalness. Here under the shadow of Belting she seemed to me raucous and ill-mannered. I made no allowances, the young never make such allowances, for the strain she must have felt in coming back to a place she hated. I did not realise that she had been drinking to give herself Dutch courage, and I was priggishly appalled by her lack of taste in bringing down so totally unsuitable a companion.

Now she spun on her flat heel, opened the door of the sports car and closed it again with a bang. "Come on then," she cried out. "Wake up inside there, it's judgement day."

As if in magical response to this call the door of the house opened and Stephen came out, followed a few moments later by David. At the same time Clarissa appeared, as she so often did, round the side of the house that led to the stables, accompanied by her bull terriers. It struck me at the time that the scene was a repetition of the one that had taken place on David's arrival, although the personalities were different. But when history repeats itself, as has been said before, it is likely to be as farce, and so it proved now, as Betty Urquhart moved forward and took hold of Stephen by both his hands.

"Brother Creep," she cried enthusiastically. "If it's not Brother Creep in person. I'd have known you anywhere. How's every little thing in the family homestead, Brother Creep?"

Stephen snatched his hands away as though they were burned. A tide of colour came up his neck and ebbed away. He tried to say something, but nothing intelligible came out.

"But where's Miles, where's my ex? Skulking inside, I suppose." She put her hands to her mouth and called his name.

"He's gone into Folkestone," I said, and with that she turned her glazed look on me.

"Run away. Afraid of seeing me again. Typical, no guts."

"He's gone to watch the cricket." I was conscious of how feeble this sounded. The words produced an unexpected reaction.

"Cricket," Max Miners said. "Is it a county game?"

"Kent and Derby."

"What luck, sweetie. We can go into this Folkestone and look at it for an hour or two, we've got time, eh? Might see your boy friend there."

"He wasn't my boy friend, idiot, I told you he was my ex." She moved free of Max's encircling arm.

"It's all the same," he said, grinning happily. He spoke beautiful English.

"I was the boy friend." That was David, speaking for the first time. He had been moving towards Betty cautiously, rather as a cat approaches somebody who may be friend or enemy. His nervous depression of the morning seemed now quite gone, and he stood smiling at her with eyes that shone. I thought, this is the moment of truth, yet even as I thought this I wondered why I should place more reliance on her word than on those of Lady W or her children. Perhaps it was because I felt, even in my revulsion of her drunkenness, that there was an unusual honesty about Betty Urquhart, so that even if she had an axe she would never grind it. If I close my eyes now I can summon up the scene as I saw it then, the hot sun shining down and giving the colours an almost Mediterranean brightness, the scarlet and grey of Betty and the black and coffee colour of her smiling companion, the little red car standing on brownish gravel, the tense white face of Stephen and the grey watchful head of Arbuthnot, the dingy brown-greyness of Clarissa's tweed and the threadbare blue of the man who called himself David Wainwright, the shiny brightness of his eyes.

"You. You're supposed to be David Wainwright?" she said as she circled him, and she said it half-questioningly, rather as though a dozen other possible David Wainwrights might be produced in course of time for her inspection.

"Oh, come on now." He spoke with assurance, but whether it came from genuine recognition I found myself unable, as often before, to determine. "I understand that this is embarrassing, but still."

"Embarrassing, hell. You're not David." Stephen made a noise that in another man could have been called a chuckle.

"How could anyone ever think so?" she asked of the blue sky, and now Stephen did speak.

"I've always said he was an impostor."

"What the hell, I mean, you're about the same height as he was, but the way you walk is different and your face is different, it's thinner altogether than David's was and I don't mean just the flesh, I mean the bone structure. David looked like a lamb and you look like a wolf and, well, I just don't see how anybody with an eye for faces could be fooled."

"If Mamma hadn't been ill she would never have been deceived," Stephen said in eager explanation, and to David: "You'd better go while you can."

David ignored him. He went up to Betty and gripped her shoulder. "You silly bitch, don't you understand what I've been through? I've been years in a Russian labour camp, do you expect me to look the same as when I slept with you?" His voice had been high and shrill, but now it dropped as he said, "Perhaps you'd like to test me out."

What happened after that was sudden, and the effect was strange, as if a film taken in slow motion had become transformed into a Keystone Cops comedy. In two strides Max Miners was beside David, had turned him round and had swung a fist at his jaw. David put up a hand to protect himself but the blow still caught him, although not with much force. He slipped, and fell on the gravel. A car, a sober black Austin saloon, crossed over the cattle grid and into the courtyard. And Clarissa let loose her bull terriers. It may be that she was hoping that they would attack David and pursue him down the drive as he ran away for ever. It may be that she let the dogs loose by accident. I never found out. What happened in fact was that they dashed unhesitatingly at Max Miners. One of them worried his beautiful coffee-coloured trousers and the other made for his body.

Betty pulled open the door of the car, got in, and cried, as though some last straw had been dropped on her heavily-laden head, "Oh hell, Max, come on, let's go."

Max was at this moment struggling with the dogs, but he managed to obey her. There was a sound of tearing cloth, a look of anguish on Max's face, and then he was in the driving seat, had started the engine, and the little red car was whirling away down the drive like, as the old phrase has it, a bat out of hell. (But why should bats in particular wish to wing their way out of hell?) The bull terriers trotted back to Clarissa and one of them deposited at her feet a patch of coffee-coloured cloth. David got to his feet. And a stiff tall bowler-hatted man got out of the Austin and looked at us as if we were all lunatics. I had seen him once before, and I recognised him. It was Humphries.

Chapter Ten

An Open Question

Humphries' arrival brought everybody back to the realities of the situation. Betty Urquhart's denunciation of the man who claimed to be David was a kind of triumph for Stephen, and somehow her subsequent abrupt departure was part of the triumph too, but such triumphs made no difference to Lady W's intention to change her will. It must have been with the feeling of a commander who knows that although he may be winning individual battles he is extremely near to losing the war, that Stephen asked Humphries to have a word with him before going upstairs.

This word was had in the drawing-room. Stephen invited me to hear it, and the inspector too, since, as he said, we were all interested. David, who might also be said to be interested, was of course not invited to this informal conference, and had conveniently disappeared. One of the maids brought in tea and biscuits, and Humphries sat there eating and drinking while Stephen, with a good deal of collar-tugging, explained the situation. The man was an impostor, he was very likely a murderer too (here Stephen made a gesture towards the inspector, who remained impassive), and surely something could be done in all the circumstances about Mamma's outrageous suggestion of changing her will.

You had only to look at Humphries to know that he was an extremely cautious man. He sipped his tea as though it might be poisoned, he nibbled at his biscuit in the manner of a mouse momentarily expecting the arrival of a large cat, he kept glancing from one to the other of us as if in hope that he might catch us in betraying some secret. When Stephen had finished he picked an invisible crumb from his lap and spoke in a solemn, plummy voice.

"I appreciate the force of what you say, Mr Wainwright, but you must understand that it would not be proper for me to give an opinion on it. My business here is solely with Lady Wainwright—"

"To draw up her new will." That was Clarissa.

Humphries hesitated, then said, "Yes, Mrs Wainwright, I understand that is why she has sent for me."

"But the man's a fraud."

"My concern as a solicitor is first that Lady Wainwright is mentally fit to make her will. Would any of you maintain otherwise?"

"She's under a delusion," Stephen said sulkily. He could see that he was losing.

"So you believe. But in other respects she is mentally capable. You agree? Very well. There is nothing to stop Lady Wainwright from leaving her money to whomsoever she chooses, and it is not my function as her solicitor to advise her on this point, unless of course she asks me." A twitch of amusement, I presumed at the thought of Lady W's asking advice on such a matter, curled his long upper lip. "Should it happen that she leaves the bulk of her estate to her son David, and you are able to show that the man who now calls himself David Wainwright is an impostor, he would not inherit."

"But that would mean a damned law suit," Stephen cried in despair.

"That is a possibility. It might depend how conclusively you could prove your case." This again seemed to give him some inner amusement.

Arbuthnot spoke for the first time. "Supposing this man is really who he claims to be, but killed Thorne. How would he stand then in relation to the inheritance?"

"A nice point," Humphries said with interest. "As you know, a man may not profit legally by his crime. But if he were David Wainwright I cannot see that his right of inheritance would be affected by the fact of his committing murder, unless it could be shown that the murder was connected with the question of inheritance."

Stephen wrung his hands as though this was more than he could bear. The door opened, and Peterson's grim face appeared. She spoke to Stephen. "Excuse me, sir. I thought I ought to tell you that *that man* is with her ladyship, and has been for half an hour."

"Oh." Stephen almost shrieked. He had been outmanoeuvred again, the enemy had turned his flank. Humphries was on his feet, and again appeared convulsed by some secret source of amusement.

"I think I should go up to Lady Wainwright now," he said. He bowed his head ceremoniously and left us.

"That's a canny man," the inspector said. "You'll not get much more than the time of day out of him."

"If you ask me he's an old fool." That was Clarissa. She added with no change of tone, "Brian and Basil need a special liver mash. I must go and see to it."

When she had gone, Stephen paced up and down. He said to Arbuthnot, "I should have thought you'd be better occupied looking for traces of Thorne's murderer than sitting here making unhelpful remarks."

The inspector took out his pipe, looked at Stephen, then deliberately filled and lighted it. "As to field work, sir, Hasty and a couple of other men are on to that, not that I think they're going to find much. I'm up here, as I told you before, because I want to know whether or not this man is David Wainwright. Putting it simply, if he is who he claims to be, he's got no obvious reason to kill Thorne."

"I tell you he's not my brother."

"I know you say so, sir, but that doesn't prove it."

"You heard that woman."

"Miss Urquhart? Yes, but I wouldn't say she was altogether convincing, would you? Apart from anything else she'd had a good deal to drink. And how did he cotton on so quickly to who she was if he's not David Wainwright, will you tell me that?"

I coughed. "She'd mentioned that Uncle Miles was once her husband. This man knows so much else that he could have put two and two together."

"If that's so he did it very quickly, you'll agree."

"You'd expect a man planning something like this to be quick-witted."

"So you would. But then, where did he get all his information from?" That silenced me. He spoke to Stephen again. "There's another possibility, d'you see, that interests me. Supposing Thorne knew something about what happened to Sullivan."

"Sullivan." Stephen spoke the name with distaste.

"Don't say you've forgotten Sullivan. Don't you remember

how you and Lady Wainwright went into the witness box and said what a nice blameless evening everybody had spent up here? You know what I'm talking about, Mr Wainwright, don't you?"

"Yes." There was sweat on Stephen's forehead.

"And lucky you were that old Greensword was in charge of it. If it had been me I'd have pushed it to the limit, understand me?"

"Hallo there." It was David. "You don't mind if I come in. That solicitor chap is with Mamma. I do hope I'm not interrupting anything. Is something the matter, Stephen?" Stephen tugged at his collar, looked as if he were about to explode, and went out of the room. "One day my brother is going to get a collar that fits him, and how will he show us he's got the fidgets then? I feel quite done for." David sat down in a chair and threw his head back against the antimacassar. He did look exhausted. The brightness had gone out of his eyes and he lay sprawled in the chair with his head back, showing his lined face, creased neck, and on his forehead the gathering and whitening of the skin that is a mark of age. I could easily see on him—or could easily think that I saw on him—the marks of the labour camp. "What were you talking about?"

"Murder," Arbuthnot said in his unemphatic voice.

"But I explained where I was last night."

"Put it this way." Arbuthnot got up and stood over David. He looked powerful, even menacing, beside the slight figure in the chair. "If you're not David Wainwright you may have had the best of reasons for killing Thorne. But if you are David then you're in line for the killing of Ted Sullivan ten years ago. Either way, it's not a nice position."

I wondered what sort of game Arbuthnot was playing.

Had he not told me a couple of hours ago that David was not involved in the Sullivan case. Or was that exactly what he had said? Whatever his game was, his words produced an effect.

"Sullivan?" said David in a dazed way.

"Come along now." Arbuthnot spoke almost coaxingly. "Your memory's not as short as that."

"Ten years ago. Surely it's all over."

"For old Greensword it may have been, but for me it's as fresh as the day it happened. Greensword was a respecter of family tradition and all that. I'm not. If I were in your shoes I'd be shaking."

Arbuthnot was leaning over David, who positively shrank back in his chair. I don't know what answer he would have made because my attention was distracted by the sound of another car drawing up outside. I began to say that that must be Doctor Foster, and then stopped before speaking the name, remembering that his arrival was supposed to be a surprise. We could hear people talking. David jerked his head up and looked from one to the other of us as though suspecting, quite rightly, that this was another trap for him. Then Stephen came in, accompanied by Foster.

Doctor Foster was dressed today for the country, in new-looking tweeds, and I found myself wondering whether he had changed from clerical grey after seeing his last morning patient. He nodded to me and to Arbuthnot, but spoke immediately to David, his manner that of doctor addressing patient as it had been with me.

"You say that you are David Wainwright."

"I am."

"As you know, some members of your family are doubtful about your claim. They have asked me to come down to verify it. I take it you have no objection to answering some questions."

David jumped up and walked quickly about the room. He ended with his back to the carved mahogany chimney-piece. "Why the hell shouldn't I object? I've been badgered and harried and smelt around ever since I came here as if I were a new specimen in a zoo. Object, indeed I should think I do object."

"But you will answer my questions," Foster repeated patiently, and I thought, if he is a fake he's going to have a rough passage now, for—it struck me—Doctor Foster's manner was really rather more like that of the Grand Inquisitor in *The Brothers Karamazov*, which I had recently been reading, than like that of a doctor. When David said that it depended what the questions were, he took this as assent, and began immediately. Perhaps I should set the scene. David stood throughout the interrogation warming himself at the non-existent fire like some Victorian squire, or like a Victorian warrior with his back to the wall, I suppose it might be said, shifting sometimes from one foot to another, or touching an ornament on the occasional table beside him. Foster also stood—feeling no doubt that by sitting down he would have lost a psychological advantage—his thick brown country shoes tapping the carpet at times to emphasise a point, his handsome head held erect so that he revealed to me, who sat in a chair facing sideways on to him, a profile of classical elegance. His manner was extremely cool and impersonal, so that he resembled a handsome Truth Machine rather than a human being. I don't know whether some mental specialists feel it right to remove themselves emotionally from their patients in this way, but the effect is forbidding. Stephen and Arbuthnot also sat, Stephen with his white face staring at the man who called himself his brother, Arbuthnot with hands folded on his stomach. So the questioning began.

"First of all, do you recognise me? Do you know who I am?"

David hesitated, then spoke. "I'll be honest and say I don't recognise you, but I'll make a guess. From the way you order people around I guess you must be Vivian Foster, right? I see I am. How are you, Vivian?"

He held out his hand, which Foster touched with two fingers, then dropped. "Where did we first meet?"

"At Oxford."

"Were we at the same college?"

"Yes, Christ Church."

"On the same staircase?"

"No."

"Who else was on your staircase?"

David paused, shook his head. "It's no good, I can't remember."

"Did we belong to any societies?"

"Hugh and I were in the OUDS, and so was Miles later on. I don't think you were. I joined the Labour Club for a year or two, but again I don't think you were a member. And of course you weren't there during the whole of my time at Oxford, you left when you decided to become a doctor. I'll tell you something, though, we once took out two girls in a punt and then went on to dinner, and we hadn't got enough to pay, remember, we had to borrow from them?" Foster was going on to another question and David interrupted, with his voice raised. "I said, do you remember? Did it happen or not? Just bloody well answer."

"Yes, it happened. Do you remember when you were involved in a crash on my motor bicycle?"

David took his time over answering. "No. What's more, I don't believe you had one. Not your style. It's a trick question."

Foster's handsome profile was impassive. "Did we meet much when we came down from Oxford?"

"Not much. You were a medical student, I was wasting time as usual."

"We didn't meet at all for two years." Foster snapped it at him as though flashing a sword through a defensive gap. "I was in Vienna."

"If you say so. I'd forgotten."

"Queer, because you wrote me at least half a dozen letters during those two years. How did they begin?"

Silence, then David was shaking his head. This was a real test, it seemed to me. If he was genuine, surely he must remember writing letters that began "Dear Vof"? Foster prompted him. "I'll help you. There was a particular way you used to begin letters to me, a particular phrase you used. You can't have forgotten it."

"I have." There was a box of chessmen on a small ornamental table to the right of David. He had opened it and now he was taking one piece after another into his hands, holding it, putting it back.

"David Wainwright wouldn't have forgotten. My second Christian name is Oswald, and you used to begin letters 'Dear Vof'."

"Did I?" He dropped a black queen on to the carpet, picked it up. While he was bending down Foster glanced at Stephen and Arbuthnot with eyebrows raised, asking without the use of words whether he should go on. Arbuthnot nodded. David straightened up.

"When did we meet next?"

"We met occasionally before the war. I can't remember." David did not look at him.

"Do you remember meeting me at a party at Nicholas Paget's house? And coming to my flat for dinner a couple of nights later? My introducing you to a Viennese girl named Magda?" David was shaking his head. "Odd that you shouldn't. I was married to Magda a few months later, and you met her several times."

It seemed to me that this was the *coup de grâce*. Stephen was staring at David with an expression of pleasure on his face, like that of the boxing fan who sees a fighter he hates punch drunk, on the ropes, at the mercy of his opponent. Foster lighted a cigarette, but he still looked at David and waited for a reply. Arbuthnot opened his eyes wide, looked hard at Foster, then half-closed them. David raised his head. There was sweat on his face.

"If I were to say that I can't remember every bloody thing—" he began, and then stopped. "Oh hell, what's the use? I just don't remember anything about Nicholas Paget or what's her name, Magda. The thing is that not one of you bastards understands what I've been through, and what it can do to a man." It was not an adequate answer, but Foster was continuing to ask questions, and somehow I felt the knockout blow had not been delivered.

"Let's come to the war. What unit was I in?"

"We were together for a while. We did our basic training at—" He looked up at the ceiling. "—at Greyswell, right? I'll tell you something about that you won't like remembering, you had a girl friend there and we used to call her the Sex Express, right? I may have forgotten about Magda but I remember the Sex Express. She existed, didn't she?"

"Yes." From where I sat Foster's features had not changed

their expression. "What pubs did we use when we were training?"

"That's not easy. I can only remember one, the Goat and Compasses, right?"

"Where did—"

David interrupted. "Damn you, is that right or not?"

"We used a pub of that name, yes."

"Then just have the goodness to say so, you sanctimonious bastard."

Foster was imperturbable. "What happened after that?"

"We were commissioned about the same time, and a couple of months later we parted company. I was Number Five Bomber Group, you were in fighters."

"Nineteen forty-four, did we meet then?" Foster waited for a reply and when it did not come, continued. "Did we meet in London on your last leave, the last one before you were shot down?" Still the other did not reply. "Come on, man, if we met it would be then. You'd just given evidence in the Sullivan affair, remember? It isn't something you'd forget. Did we meet?"

David glared at him. "Yes, we met. The news of Hugh's death had come through. We had a night out. I was trying to forget it."

"All right," Foster said suddenly. The tension of his body relaxed, I could see even sideways that he was smiling, he put out his hand. David took it. Stephen's eyes were popping out of his head in surprise.

"What—" he began, stopped, and began again. "Do you mean to say—"

Foster turned to him, a solemn specialist giving his opinion. "I can't be absolutely certain, but I'm prepared to accept that this is my friend David Wainwright."

"*Accept* him." I thought Stephen would choke.

"At first I was very doubtful. He's changed a lot, but then after his experiences that's not surprising. But his answers to the questions have pretty well convinced me."

"Your wife—Magda. He didn't know about her."

Foster laughed. "I haven't got a wife, let alone one named Magda. If this were not David, wouldn't he have said yes, he remembered her, and even invented a detail or two? That was one trap, and the motor bicycle was another. He came through them both."

Arbuthnot interrupted. "There is a technique that intelligent criminals use. When you're in doubt, keep silent or say you don't know. Fortunately there aren't too many intelligent criminals."

"Of course, of course." Foster waved one well-shaped hand. "That's why I say I can't be positive. I am offering an opinion, not stating a fact."

"The letters," Stephen said desperately. "He didn't remember how he wrote to you."

"A good point," Foster conceded, lecturer to student. "But after all, it's been a long time, and he's been through the mill." David looked down at his hands, each of which contained a chessman. He put them back into the box as Foster said casually, "By the way, there's one other thing. That old appendicitis scar, you won't mind if I have a look at that?"

David stopped, his body rigid with some kind of excitement. "Appendicitis scar."

"Just a matter of form, old man."

"Why the hell should I let you see it?" I had the impression that if the chessmen had been still in David's hand he would have thrown them at Foster. "You come down and put questions to me as if I were in the dock, trick questions at that—*and* there's a policeman ready to take a note of anything I say that's out of line—and then you say 'Come on, David, get your trousers down and show us your scar'. I'm not bloody well having any, I can tell you that."

"I'm very sorry." Foster magisterially waved aside the remarks that Stephen was itching to make. "Of course you're perfectly within your rights—"

"Thank you."

"There is no need for sarcasm. I was going to add that this is bound to affect my feelings."

"Why? Why should I consent to being humiliated?"

"It's up to you," Foster said, and Arbuthnot spoke at the same time.

"This seems to be a chance of clearing things up once and for all. I should have thought you'd like to take it."

A muscle in David's cheek was twitching. "Let me tell you, my body's all scars, not just appendicitis."

Foster said nothing more. His face was a handsome mask. Stephen could not restrain himself. "Don't you understand, Foster, he's got no scar, you've called his bluff, that's all you had to do, he wouldn't dare—"

He stopped, for David had nodded to Foster. They began to move out of the room. Stephen stood with his mouth open. "Where are you going?"

"I've decided to let Vivian examine me. But I'm not having the rest of you there."

"But why shouldn't I—" Stephen began, and then faltered. He was leaving a great many sentences unfinished. Foster spoke, as always with that air of saying the last word on the subject.

"It seems to me entirely reasonable that David should want this examination to take place in private. If I may say so, Wainwright, I am here at your request, or at the request of your ambassador Barrington. If you don't trust me to perform the examination, then say so." Stephen was silenced. "You have no objection, Inspector?"

"Why should I object?" It seemed to me that Arbuthnot was enjoying himself. They were not away more than five minutes. When they came back a look at David's smiling face was enough to tell me what had happened, but Stephen had to know the worst. "Well?" he said. "Well?"

"The scar is there."

"You remember it, do you? It's in the same place?"

"The scar is there," Foster repeated.

I had no reason to like Stephen, but I felt sorry for him then. He looked about him, ran a hand through his hair, and went out of the room as though he could not bear any more.

"And never called me brother," David murmured. The phrase jarred me by what seemed its callousness. I did not approve of Stephen's attitude, but was this all that David could say in his moment of victory? It seemed to me that there was a lack of warmth in the goodbyes exchanged between David and Foster, although I hope I have made it clear that Foster's emotional temperature seemed to me at all times sub-normal. It was not surprising that there were no emotional farewells, but it did seem to me a little strange that they made no arrangements for meeting in London, and that there seemed more constraint in Foster's manner than there had been before the examination. It was Arbuthnot who walked out with him to the courtyard, and they stood there talking for a minute or two beside Foster's car. David watched them through the window, his hands picking up little knick-knacks and putting them down again. He spoke, and his voice was high-pitched.

"I can't take much more of this. I've had enough of it, I'm not going to answer any more questions from anybody."

He went out of the drawing-room, and after a minute I followed him, reaching the courtyard in time to see the Austin Princess going out of the drive.

Arbuthnot had his pipe going again, and its blue smoke drifted upwards into the air, yet he looked nervously defiant about it even out here, as though afraid that Lady W might pop out at any moment and rebuke a member of the lower orders for smoking near the premises. He said with some satisfaction, "Quite an afternoon for the Wainwright clan. David is really David, or is he? His lady friend says no, his doctor friend says a doubtful yes, so who do we believe?"

His lady friend! I had forgotten Betty Urquhart in the stress of Foster's examination and its result, but now I caught hold of the inspector's last phrase. What made him think Foster's identification was doubtful?

"Because it was. You saw his manner afterwards, and I asked him what he had found. There's an appendicitis scar, and it's much in the place he remembers, but it seemed to him that it was too recent. And the man's body is a mass of scars, he was telling the truth about that, and a couple of them partly cover the appendicitis scar. So really the verdict is not proven, as you might put it."

"Why didn't he say so?"

He chuckled. "That's the sort of man he is, d'you see. He can recognise a nasty mess, and he wants to keep away from it. He pretty well told me as much out here, said he didn't want to be involved any further. That's the upper class for you all over." I was not flattered by the fact that he seemed to identify me with his own class, whatever he considered that to be. "I think I might have another word with Master David."

"He said he'd had enough, he wouldn't answer any more questions."

"Ah well, time enough. I must be getting along, they'll be looking for me at the station. I might get corrupted here, might get to envying all these smart cars." He patted his old but well-preserved vehicle.

"Why did you talk about the—the Sullivan affair—in that threatening way, when you told me David had nothing to do with it?"

"I didn't exactly say that, did I?" He got into the car, looked at me consideringly. "Here's a bit of information you can pass on. We've heard from the Paris police. They've checked at the address from which that original letter to Lady Wainwright was written, and a man resembling your David Wainwright had been living there all right, under the name of Stiver. But he hadn't been there for a year as he said, only for a few weeks. What d'you make of that?"

I made nothing of it. The car started first time, and he was away. The setting sun in the blue sky was red as blood.

Chapter Eleven

The Last Time

I remember dinner that night very well, for it was the last meal David ate in the house, and the last time I saw Lady W alive. She came down leaning on David's arm, and it was noticeable that ever since his return she had become weaker. She drank only a mouthful of soup, and refused the roast chicken, but she dominated the dinner-table—that is to say, the family—as she had done ever since I had known her.

"I had Humphries here today," she said, as though we might have been unaware of it. "And you know what he came for, I told you, I've changed my will." David was sitting next to her as before, and she patted his hand. He looked as if the meat in his mouth might choke him. "At the same time, I don't want you to think, any of you, that your names have been left out. You are all mentioned. I still have a sense of justice." She paused, crumbled bread which she did not eat. "That policeman was here, I saw you talking to him in the courtyard, Christopher. He was smoking. I trust that he didn't do so indoors. A jumped-up little man," she said severely, although it was not accurate to call Arbuthnot little. "The post-war generation," she added with equal inaccuracy.

There was silence, broken by Uncle Miles. His bald pate had been made rosy by the sun. "A very lively afternoon's cricket," he said. "A beautiful innings by Phebey."

Lady W turned upon him her still-devastating eye, and as she spoke I realised that although she might be in bed all day the intelligence service provided by Peterson was a good one. "You missed your former wife this afternoon. She came here, drunk of course, accompanied by a Negro. Was it at your invitation?"

Uncle Miles managed to observe the truth, although not the whole truth. "No, certainly I didn't invite her."

"I am glad to hear it. She came uninvited." Her glance moved from one to the other of us. "Peterson tells me that one of your dogs attacked her companion, Clarissa. I always thought that those dogs had a use."

The chicken was succeeded by a chocolate mousse. "We had another visitor," Lady W went on. "I believe he was an old friend of yours, David."

"Yes, Doctor Foster," David muttered. He seemed in low spirits.

"Vivian Foster, isn't that right? I remember him coming here when your dear father was alive, rather a conceited boy. Did you ask him down? No? Strange that we should have these uninvited visitors so soon after your return." She looked round the table. "That policeman stayed an unconscionably long time. Did he favour any of you with information about his investigation into the death of poor Thorne?"

Nobody said anything and I became irritated, as I had been before, by their reluctance to annoy her. "I don't think he came about that."

"Indeed?" She gave me a nearly-annihilating glance.

"He's interested in David's life in Paris." I addressed David.

"The French police have been making inquiries at the address the letter came from. They say you were only there a few weeks."

If I had had any expectations about the effect of this remark, what happened would have exceeded them. David pushed aside his mousse, got up from the table, and said in the high-pitched voice I had heard that afternoon, "Excuse me, Mamma. I'm not going to stand this, I'm not going to be questioned any more." He flung down his napkin and went out.

"Poor boy, he feels the strain," Lady W said as she looked after him, and I wish I had known, I wish I knew now, what she was thinking. Looking back, I am sure that David's return was a great joy to her, but how much was it blended with a belief that he had come home simply in the hope that she would change her will, as she had done? I don't know. In these last weeks of her life she was living in a world of fantasy, one in which she compelled reality to conform to the shapes made by her imagination. She wished to find the son she had lost and she would accept nothing less. That is what I think now, although I cannot be sure of it.

She left us and went to her room a few minutes after David's departure, saying that she felt tired, but refusing help in getting to her room. I wish I could think of something memorable to say about this last view of her, for more than anybody else she had changed the course of my life, but I can recall nothing but the authoritative nod she gave as she slowly rose from the table, and my feeling of regret that her white hair should be again so limp and tangled.

I did not want to hear Stephen and Clarissa lamenting in detail the injustice done them, nor to hear Miles joining in, so I left them and went to my Thomas Lovell. There I tried to write a poem, but got no further than the first two lines:

> *The bloody values of an evening sky,*
> *The dark calligraphy of clouds*

I tried to read Max Beerbohm, but could not concentrate on him. I lay on the bed and took the leftermost book on the shelf beside me. I had read somewhere a practice recommended for aspiring men of letters, that of keeping beside their beds a shelf of books taken at random, one of which would be looked at every evening and then either discarded or more thoroughly investigated on the following day. The idea assumed both leisure and the existence of a library from which to make the random selection, and both of these existed for me out of term time, when I gathered an armful of books from the Pam Moor or one of the corridors, and went through them. The book I took down was an elegant edition of Donne's *Songs and Sonets*, and this in itself shows the random nature of my chosen armful, for I knew them well. I had the book open, when there was a light tap at the door and David came in.

"I thought I should find you here." He looked about him. "You've certainly made this very individual."

I waited for him to say why he had come, but he seemed in no hurry. "You do a lot of writing. You're hoping to take that up, aren't you?"

"Yes."

"I want—would you do something for me, without telling anybody else, I mean?"

"I don't know. You'd better tell me what it is." I swung my legs off the bed and looked at him. His movements were jerky, unco-ordinated, and a muscle was twitching angrily in his cheek. I remembered the almost impertinent assurance with which he had greeted Betty Urquhart, and it struck me that he was subject to extraordinarily sudden changes of mood.

"I don't think I can stick this much longer. Stephen and Miles hate me, they'd rather I'd stayed dead. If I'd known what it was going to be like—"

"You would have done?"

"I think I would, yes."

"You haven't told me what you want me to do."

"Carry a message, a letter, I mean. Deliver a letter for me tomorrow morning, that's all. Will you do that?"

"Where to?"

"A place in Filehurst. It wouldn't take you long."

"Why can't you do it yourself?"

"Reasons. I don't know why you ask all these questions, *you've* got no cause to be against me." There was something pettish yet pathetic about this, and there was a rising note of hysteria in his voice as he went on. "I really don't think I can stay, I can't endure it."

"What's this letter to do with you staying?"

"I can't tell you. I thought you would trust me. You like her, don't you, Mamma, I mean?" I did not reply, but he went on as though I had said yes. "Then you can understand, if it weren't for her I wouldn't stay another hour to be insulted. When she's so ill, I don't like to leave her."

"You must have seen a great change in her."

"Ghastly, yes. Yet do you know, essentially she still looks just the same to me as she did ten years ago."

It was not with any idea of testing him, but simply because I had been reading "The Undertaking" when he came in, that I quoted:

> But he who loveliness within
>   Hath found, all outward loathes,
> For he who colour loves, and skin,
>   Loves but their oldest clothes.

Yet he took it as a trap and so it was in effect, although not in intention. "What's that?" he cried. "What is it you're saying, what do you mean?"

"It's a quotation. From Donne's *Songs and Sonets*. The book you kept with you for years in Russia and brought back, remember?"

For a moment there was in his eyes the terror of a hunted animal. Then he said shrilly, "You're like all the rest. Trying to trick me. I was a fool ever to think I could trust you." He seemed about to say something more. Then he pawed inadequately at the air with his hands, turned and left the room. When he had gone I knew that, whatever people like Foster might say, and in spite of Lady W, for me the die was cast. It had been a trivial incident, yet it was decisive. I should never again believe that he was David Wainwright.

It must have been some time after nine when he left me, and it was half an hour later that, on my way to the lavatory, which was some distance from my room, I heard him speaking on the telephone. It was a peculiarity of the sentry box that, although what was said in it could not be heard by any listener on the ground floor, the top of the box was made of some sort of thin wood that acted as a sounding box. Standing as I was in the gallery above, I could not fail to hear every word. I will not deny that when I heard David's voice I stood still and listened.

"What?" I heard him say. "What do you mean? Are you absolutely sure of that? Didn't he leave any message? Are you sure that he left no message for Mr Wainwright?" There was a pause and then he spoke in a voice from which all vibrancy, all tone, had vanished. "If he should come in, tell him I called. He'll know the number. Thank you." The telephone made its usual jangling sound when he replaced it, and then

I heard him close the door of the sentry box, stand outside it for a moment, and begin to ascend the stairs. He came up them like an old man.

I could not sleep that night. Eyes wide, staring up at the invisible ceiling, I speculated. Who could the telephone call have been made to, when David had said that he had no friends in this country? Perhaps the call had been made to somebody abroad, in Paris say? But I believed that I did not believe this, that in my heart I knew the call had been made to somebody nearby. I do not know why I should have been so certain of this, except that one uses a different tone of voice for local calls from the tone one uses for calls made at a greater distance. The longer the distance the louder the voice, I said to myself drowsily, and then, always with my eyes open, it should be understood, I elaborated in my mind the voice that would be used for somebody in Edinburgh, in Leeds, Derby, London, Maidstone. Edinburgh would be an almost continuous shout, Maidstone comparatively a whisper. What sort of voice would a spy use? And, tangling myself up like Uncle Miles, I varied this by saying: what sort of you would a voice spy? This is the last moment before falling asleep, I said to myself, and as often before falling asleep the truth will become suddenly plain to you. The trick after that is to hold on to it. In that last moment before sleep I understood everything. David was a spy, a spy in the service of Ulfheim, but Ulfheim knew that the game was up and had left the hotel that was their usual meeting place. Ulfheim, disguised as a clergyman, was moving about the country and was prepared to give up spying in favour of the sale of pornographic postcards, he was proposing to get himself appointed vicar of Appledore like Trebitsch Lincoln, and once appointed would make up his dispensations in plain packets which included the photographs, but Arbuthnot in the guise of a wholesaler in these photographs was setting a trap for him. From his suitcase, Ulfheim produced *something* with long trailing wires…

With an effort I jerked myself awake, to see Stephen standing in the doorway, white-faced as ever. He was carrying a big torch which he shone directly into my eyes. "Get up, that swine's set fire to the house, he knows he's finished," he said hoarsely. As I scrambled out of bed he said urgently that there was no time to get dressed. Why was he carrying a torch, I asked, and he snapped back that the electricity had been cut off, and that I shouldn't waste time in asking silly questions. I noticed that although he too was wearing pyjamas and dressing-gown he had on his stiff white collar. Outside Clarissa was shouting something confusing about her dogs. I heard knocking, and when I asked Stephen what it was, he said that Miles was trying to break down that man's bedroom door. I said to Stephen that I must save my pictures. "Don't be a fool," he said scornfully. "How can you save them? If I turn off the torch you can't see where they are." He suited his action to the words, and the room was completely dark. I cried out and put my hand to where the light switch should have been, but there was no switch, no way of obtaining light…

With an effort I jerked myself awake. My hand was on the switch. I pressed it, and the room was flooded with light. My pyjamas were clammy with sweat. I looked round the room. There was no sign of Stephen, no smell of smoke. A nightmare, that was all.

I looked at my watch. The time was half past four. It was nonsense, then, to think that I had not slept. I had been asleep and something had wakened me, but what? I got out of bed and went across to the window. Birds were calling, a wind was blowing, it was almost dawn. Thirty feet away a wicket gate that led into the kitchen garden was flapping open and shut. The noise it made was no doubt the knocking I had heard in my dream. But the wicket gate was always kept shut, and surely it would have woken me before had it been knocking all night? As I stared at it, an idea came into my mind. I put on my dressing-gown, a gaily-coloured one made of Chinese silk embroidered with dragons, and padded along the corridors to David's room. When there was no answer to my knock, I turned the door handle. His bed had been used, but he was not in the room.

It was what I had expected, and I did not really need the confirmation given me when I opened the great mahogany wardrobe and saw that his clothes and the single case he had brought were gone. The man who called himself David Wainwright had vanished, and I had not the least doubt that he would never return. He had become increasingly alarmed by the police investigation, he had become aware of the pitfalls that lay around him on all sides even in such matters as identifying a quotation from Donne, he had made an unsuccessful attempt to get in touch with the man for whom he had been working, and when this failed he had given up, his nerve strained beyond endurance. Perhaps he had gone to bed still meaning to face things out, but during the night had decided that the threat of a murder charge was too much for him. Or perhaps he had made up his mind to run immediately after the abortive telephone call, and had then chosen his moment. Either way it was over, we had won (I say "we" for I identified myself as a matter of course with the rest of the family), and there was no good reason for the disappointment I felt. He had gone, but he had left unresolved mysteries behind him. I looked round the room in the hope of finding explanations.

It was called the Blue Room because the walls were painted a most unattractive shade of peacock blue, and it was generally reserved for guests. A school friend of mine who had stayed in it had said that it looked as if it contained an assortment of things unsold at a country auction. I had been annoyed by the remark at the time, but later saw that it was apposite. There was the huge wardrobe, an equally monstrous tallboy, one of the biggest chests of drawers I have ever seen, and a gigantic cheval glass. The bed was a curious and in its way rather handsome affair, a true Victorian folly with a rosewood bedhead into which was let fragments of mother-of-pearl. They were pretty to look at but must, I reflected, have been uncomfortable for anybody given to reading or breakfasting in bed. There was a revolving bookcase beside the bed on one side, and on the other an ornate cupboard with a circular front, of the kind that contains a chamberpot. I poked about the room in an aimless way, looking for something that would give me a clue to the identity and character of the man who had stayed in it, searching for a secret drawer in the tallboy, for something left in the chest of drawers. I had no luck until I came to the chamberpot cupboard, and then I did not at first understand the meaning of the eye-dropper, needle and bent spoon that I found. Since the inveterate reader of thrillers is likely to be more perceptive than I was then and would be bored by a detailed account of my thought processes, let me say at once that these are the tools of the drug addict, and not simply of the addict but of the mainliner who obtains an extra kick by injecting heroin directly into the vein. When I had understood this I saw why total self-assurance, in the presence of Betty Urquhart for instance, had alternated with hysterical nervousness in David, as I shall continue to call him. I guessed also that part of the reason for Foster's reserve after examining him was discovery of the tiny tell-tale punctures on arms or buttocks that reveal the addict. This, no doubt, was something which he had told Arbuthnot but which Arbuthnot had not told me.

I am running ahead of myself, for I worked out the meaning of the spoon, needle and eye-dropper later after much thought, whereas the meaning of my other discovery was plain within half a minute. After looking at the chamberpot cupboard I investigated the revolving bookcase, which contained historical novels by Maurice Hewlett, Stanley Weyman and Conan Doyle. As I turned the bookcase, however, I saw that a book in a brown paper cover had been stuffed behind the Weymans. I took it out and looked at the title: *Prisoners of the Soviets*. True Tales of the Labour Camps. Collected by E G Clapham. The book was divided into chapters, each referring to one case, and they had such headings as "The Real Face of Socialism" by R Zinkowski, and "Tragedy of a Polish Resistance Fighter" by Camp Inmate No. R813724. A piece of paper was inserted in the book at a chapter called "An Englishman's Disillusionment in the Promised Land," by Gerald Flame. Certain passages were marked heavily in pencil. The first of them read:

> The routine of the camp varied little. We were woken each day at six, and at half past had the first of our two meals, which generally consisted either of a watery soup with bits of gristle from some unidentifiable animal floating about in it, or a thick one absolutely stiff with a very coarse and tasteless kind of lentil. Cherno, the wit of our

hut, called the thick soup wallpaper paste and the thin one rainwater flavoured with bird droppings. This was followed by a hunk of stale bread, with a bit of tough sausage sometimes as a treat. One day somebody broke a tooth on a piece of bone in the sausage and we adopted Cherno's name for it, rock sausage.

I turned to the other marked passages. They all resembled bits of David's story. I will transcribe one more:

The conduct of the guards varied, but on the whole they were less brutal than the Nazis. I shall always remember one of them, a boy with an almost completely shaven head whose name was unpronounceable, so that like everybody else I called him Ivan. He was always slipping us little things like cigarettes or fragments of chocolate, which must have come out of his own allowance. One day, when we were working in the fields after one of our nightly discussions about escape, I decided to test out Cherno's theory that anybody could get away easily without being noticed. I began to work farther and farther away from my companions, and from Ivan, who was our guard in my section. Eventually I was out of sight of everybody, and I began to think that Cherno was right, when Ivan suddenly appeared from nowhere. He shook his head, said *"Niet,"* and pointed to the illimitable expanse of plain that extended in every direction. Then, as if fearing that I still might not understand, he said with a great effort, "Nix," and after a pause, "No good."

As I read on it became clear that David had learned parts of this chapter almost by heart. Only parts, for Flame's story did not really much resemble the one David had given himself. He was a British civilian, in Germany when the war began, who was arrested as a spy, sent to a concentration camp and then in 1941 handed over by the Germans to the Russians, who put him into a labour camp from which he was released in 1948. David had taken what was useful in Flame's story and supplemented it with other material, like the account of how a guard stamped on his fingers and broke the bones.

I read this chapter sitting on the bed. When I had finished I realised that I held in my hand the positive proof that everybody had been looking for, the proof that David was an impostor. What should I do with it? Show Stephen and Miles? I had no sympathy for David, yet I felt that I could not endure the mean delight of Stephen and Clarissa's doggy comments, nor could I bear the way in which they would conspire to make sure that Lady W changed her will again, without making themselves too conspicuous in arranging it. I should in any case have to show it to Arbuthnot, but I rebelled even against this in my mind, saying to myself that Arbuthnot had kept things from me so that I was under no obligation to him, but really feeling a sense of disappointment that the chase was over and understanding Stevenson's maxim that it is better to travel hopefully than to arrive.

While I was thinking about this I noticed that the bit of paper had dropped out of the book and lay on the carpet. It was a sheet of hotel writing paper, with an address at the top: Hôtel Oeil d'Or, 18 rue Mallarmé, Paris, VIIe. I knew then what I was going to do. I was not going to tell anybody about the book. I was going to Paris.

Chapter Twelve

Paris

In the forty-eight hours after the discovery I made in *Prisoners of the Soviets* I must have been suffering from a severe attack of the detective fever, running the highest possible temperature. That is the only way in which I can account for my actions. I ought to make clear, what you have perhaps understood already, that I am not adventurous by nature although I have as much curiosity as most people. I see that I have not described my appearance and perhaps, even at this late point, I ought to do so. Looking the other day at a snapshot Elaine took of me a few weeks after the whole affair was over, I saw a solemn young man with an egg-shaped face topped by long lank hair, wearing rather consciously aesthetic clothes and not quite knowing what to do with his hands, the kind of young man you would expect to be perfectly at home looking up footnotes to Nietzsche for his Ph.D. And in fact that is very much what it was like, so how could it possibly have happened that on Saturday I was on the Channel boat from Folkestone to Calais standing in the bows beside a young woman, the two of us dedicated to solving the Sullivan Mystery or the problem of the Claimant? It was the detective fever, no doubt about it.

I made my preparations in the early hours of Saturday. I had enough money for the fare, and also for a couple of days in Paris. I caught the first bus into Folkestone before anybody else was up. After some hesitation I left a note in my room, addressed to Uncle Miles, saying that David had gone and that I knew he was an impostor. I added a PS which seemed to me impressively casual: "Gone to France for a couple of days, back on Monday." In Folkestone I had breakfast and telephoned the *Record*. The office boy assistant gave me Elaine's address, after telling me that she was not on duty this Saturday. She lived in a two-roomed flat over a shop, and when I told her what had happened she was almost as excited as I was.

"You're going over there." She looked at me with new respect. "But what are you going to do?"

"Look for Stiver. First in that hotel he wrote from, and then at the one on the bit of paper he left in the book."

She had been eating breakfast in her dressing-gown. Now she poured another cup of coffee and put on her spectacles. "Not much to go on," she said severely.

I shrugged. After my discoveries I really felt that I needed nothing to go on, I had such a brilliant intuitive capacity to perceive the truth. She asked whether I knew Paris, and I reluctantly admitted that I didn't. She remarked that she knew it, and conveyed an intimacy which was far from the reality of her two visits there in a school party. There was silence. Then she said, "Would there be another place on that boat?"

I knew then that I had hoped she would say something like that, although I would not have suggested it for the world. She added, with a casualness equal to my own, that she happened to be doing nothing that weekend. At half past ten we were on the boat, and by mid-afternoon we were in Paris. For the first time I was abroad.

Abroad: it is a word that holds little magic for me now— How can I convey what it meant then? The ridiculous ritual of going through customs, the clothes of the porters at Calais, the strange cushioning of the railway carriages, the posters which advertised unknown products, all seemed to me inexpressibly romantic. I felt—I suppose in a way it was part of the detective fever—as if I were living in a fairy tale, and this feeling was not changed by the dreary blankness of much of the French countryside and the sameness of the small towns. I simply sat and stared out of the carriage window most of the way to Paris, wrapped in a daze of pleasure that had no logical basis. Elaine said afterwards that I behaved as though I were drunk, and that when she spoke to me she received no rational reply, so that in the end she gave up conversation and practised her French on the other people in the carriage, telling them that I was not very well.

Luckily for both of us I had more or less recovered my reason by the time we reached the Gare du Nord. The first shock of *abroad* had worn off, and although I do not think I was fully responsible for my actions during any of this time in Paris I was able to talk sensibly and to make coherent plans in spite of the fact that one part of me, and the part I felt to be most acutely sensitive, was aching with the experience of abroad, and was trying to tell me that our reason for being here was a triviality.

We had neither of us eaten since breakfast. We went to a little café near the station, one of several that advertised lunch for 35 francs including wine. We could hardly have made a worse choice, for the food was very much what we might have got for a little less money in England, watery soup, tough fried chicken and chips and a small piece of cheese. The wine was a tiny carafe of rough, red stuff that provided a glass for each of us. Elaine made a face as she drank, but to me it tasted like nectar.

We had bought a map of Paris at the airport, and studied it over coffee, or rather Elaine studied it and made practical comments which I took in as well as I could, although they did not fully penetrate my dream of abroad. The rue Bavaine was in the 6th arrondissement, and she decided that we should go by Métro. I suggested that we ought first to find a hotel and deposit the cases, or at least check them somewhere, but she was all for going straight away to the Hôtel les deux Pigeons. Perhaps we might stay there, she suggested.

So we went out again into the Paris sunlight, and I remembered some lines of T S Eliot:

> *Yet with these April sunsets, that somehow recall*
> *My buried life, and Paris in the Spring,*
> *I feel immeasurably at peace, and find the world*
> *To be wonderful and youthful, after all.*

It does not need to be April, I thought, it can just as well be a sunny day in July, and my pleasure was enhanced rather than diminished when we went down into the darkness of the Métro, dingy and noisy but still exciting. We came out at St Germain des Prés, walked along the Boulevard St Germain and into the network of narrow streets that lead off it in the direction of the Quai des Grandes Augustines. I exclaimed as we passed the Deux Magots and would have liked to go in there, it looked so much like home to a member of the Æsthetes' Group, but Elaine pulled me past it. She must at this point have wondered what use I should be in our quest, combining as I did the qualities of a tourist and a sleepwalker.

The rue Bavaine was a narrow cul-de-sac and the Hôtel les deux Pigeons, a slit of doorway between two shops, was not prepossessing. Elaine strode in ahead of me, to a small, dark hall illuminated by an electric lamp of the lowest possible wattage—its miserable light brought back to me thoughts of the daylight lamps at Belting. "Hallo," she shouted, and I echoed her, adopting without positive intention what I imagined to be a French accent, the aitch dropped: "'Allo." A door ahead of us opened and a collarless man with a three-day growth of beard came out, glared at us, and let loose a volley of French.

At this point, with the mention of my accent and that volley of French, I approach a similar problem to that confronting film makers who set their stories in foreign countries. Are the natives to speak their own language most of the time and so be unintelligible to the audience, or is everybody after a token "*Bonjour*" or "*Buenas dias*" or "*Bom dia*" to settle into good sound English or American? French had been one of my poorest subjects at school, a fact I regretted chiefly because I found so much difficulty in reading Baudelaire, and Elaine's fluent French was, as we discovered, largely incomprehensible to Frenchmen. If I were to describe in accurate detail our encounters in Paris, a large part of them would consist of our attempts to make ourselves understood, a procedure that is all very well in a stage farce but is liable to become boring when repeated in a book. I have settled, after some thought, for cutting out our lengthy confusions in French and pidgin-French, and for setting them down in English.

Our most serious troubles came, in fact, with the collarless gentleman. I couldn't grasp a word he said, although Elaine answered him at equal speed it was obvious that they were making as little contact as ships moving on parallel courses.

At sight of our cases he assumed that we wanted to stay, and it was with great difficulty that we stopped him from seizing them and taking them upstairs. Elaine went on talking, he produced with an air of triumph a filthy old register and a pen, it was all very French farcical. Then the name "Stiver" got through to him. He gave a jump as though he had been pricked by a needle, and began to shoo us towards the entrance. At a moment when our defeat looked inevitable this door opened, and a handsome young man appeared. Further volleys of French were exchanged between him and the collarless man, and then the young man said in English: "What is it you wish?"

It seemed time for me to say something. "We are friends of Monsieur Stiver. We are trying to find him."

"Gone to England."

"Ah, but he has left England and come back to Paris." I found it difficult not to emulate the young man by speaking English with a French accent, and I saw Elaine stifle a smile, but the young man himself seemed to find nothing strange about it. He gave a nod to the collarless man, who shrugged and retreated behind the door from which he had emerged. The young man thrust out his hand. "Durcet," he said, and jerked a thumb backwards. "My father. You want to stay 'ere? Want a room?"

"We are not quite sure yet," Elaine said. "And we should want two rooms."

He gave her one glance and turned back to me. "Why do you want Jean?"

"Jean?"

"Jean Stiver." I ought to say that whereas I pronounced the name with a long "i" he of course pronounced it as a Frenchman, "Steevay." He went on, "We have had trouble already."

"With the police, I know. But we are not the police."

"You are his friends, you want something, eh? We don't talk 'ere." Now he was smiling. He led the way outside. In the street he looked much less handsome. His complexion was bad and his teeth discoloured. We followed him into a café three doors down the street. Here it was even darker than it had been in the hotel. There was a little bar and some sort of canned music. The place was empty except for the man behind the bar and an old man half-asleep at a table. Durcet took us to the back of the café where it was darkest, went to the bar and came back with three glasses of beer. He set them down and said again, "You want something?"

"We want to know about Jean. He may be in trouble."

"Yes?" He took out a packet of Gaulloises, offered them to us, lighted one himself. "You too?"

"No. We want to help him. How long did he stay with you?"

"A few weeks, five, six."

"Did you know him before that?"

"I never saw him before. Somebody told him to come to us, you understand, we could get what he wants. You want that too?"

Elaine answered. "If the price is right."

He turned to her, as if in relief at having things out in the open. "Price is okay."

She said slowly, "Jean told us that when he was cut off he tried to kill himself."

He stared at her, "Ah, shit, that was nothing. He had no money, so he gets—credit." He searched for the word, came out with it proudly. "But still he's got no money, so—"

"You cut off supplies."

"It was nothing. Just an accident, nothing. Then this

friend came, everything was okay. Perhaps Jean is with him now."

"What friend?"

"A fat man, smiling, he has a gold tooth. He paid for everything." He opened his mouth and tapped one of his own decaying teeth. Elaine and I looked at each other. Ulfheim. Durcet saw the look, and realised that he had made a mistake. He stood up, between us and the door. "You don't want the stuff, what the hell is it you want, eh?"

I said to Elaine, "I think we should go." I hope I looked more composed than I felt. Durcet put his hand to his narrow hip. I could not positively say that I saw the glint of steel in the dark little room, but I felt sickeningly sure that he had a knife.

Elaine put on her spectacles. She said in a voice not loud but firm, "Sit down." Durcet stood for a moment, hand upon hip as though posing. Then, surprisingly, he sat down. "You had better know the facts. I am a journalist, he is working with me. Jean Stiver came to England and has disappeared. My paper has sent me here to find him. We are not interested in anything except the story, nothing at all, you understand."

"*A journalist.*" Durcet relaxed and smiled. "That's okay."

She clicked her fingers at me, I got three more beers and the crisis was over. We got a little more from Durcet, just about enough to justify buying him a beer. I was surprised that he was ready to talk. I did not understand then, although Elaine already knew from experience, that for many people a journalist's is a glamorous occupation. People say things to journalists that they would not say to their friends, because they catch a whiff of immortality, which for them means their name in the paper. Of course there are a lot of people whose feelings in the presence of journalists are quite the reverse of this, but Durcet was not one of them. Once assured that we were not interested in his drug-pushing, he was delighted by the idea that Stiver had done something sufficiently sinister to bring us to France.

He told us that Stiver had come to the hotel one day and taken a room. He had had no visitors except the man with the gold tooth, whose name Durcet did not know. Nor did he know what they had talked about. Why had Stiver chosen the Hôtel les deux Pigeons? Durcet strongly hinted, without positively committing himself, that Stiver had known it was a place where he could easily get a fix when he wanted it. He had gone off most days in the mornings and come back in the late afternoon, but Durcet did not know whether he had gone to a job. As far as he knew, Stiver had received no letters, but the two had talked together occasionally. On the last occasion Stiver had said he was going back to England, where he came from, and that he was going to be rich.

As he told this story, smoking several Gaulloises and pausing every so often to get a phrase straight, his manner became almost confidential. When he had finished, he said, "That's all? You don't want to try—"

"No." Elaine took off her spectacles. Without them she looked five years younger and very appealing, and it was obvious that Durcet thought so too.

"Lots of other things in Paris to see. Shows. You like to write about them?"

"I don't think so," I said. I was rather humiliated by the way in which Elaine had taken over from me.

"A place Jean used to go." He took a card from his pocket and put it into the pocket of Elaine's raincoat. As he did so his hand touched her thigh. "If you change your mind, baby." He rose with the smoothness of a snake, raised a hand to us and was gone.

I was prepared to visit another café, preferably the Deux Magots, sit watching people go by and discuss the implications of what we had discovered, but Elaine would have none of it. She insisted that we must go at once to the Hôtel Oeil d'Or, and of course she was perfectly right, it was what we had come for, but now that I was in Paris I was inclined to think that this evening we ought to enjoy ourselves and that tomorrow would be time enough to take up the chase, if one could call it that. But I didn't like even to suggest such backsliding thoughts to Elaine and I simply stood looking about me, sniffing the Parisian air, while Elaine studied the map. Then we dived again into the Métro. Just before we did so she tapped the cases standing in front of us and said, "Don't forget we need somewhere to stay for the night before we go out on the town." Something in the way she said it made me remember the touch of Durcet's hand upon her thigh. Should I even dare to make so bold a gesture?

Down into the Métro again, then, and a longer journey, which involved a change at Montparnasse and a walk through an interminable series of tunnels. This was the rush hour and we were jammed into a jolting, swaying train, crammed with men and women whose clothes, I could not help noticing, were very much shabbier than they would have been in a London underground train. Those damned cases were the cause of more trouble. One enormously fat man in a ragged pullover expressed what was obviously a strong objection to their presence in the carriage, half a dozen others chimed in, and the cases were furiously patted and prodded. Elaine, of course, was not silent. She seemed to be maintaining our perfect right to occupy space with the suitcases, "*espace*" cropped up continually in the flow of words, and it seemed to me that in the end the discussion shifted away from the question of the cases altogether, on to some sort of argument about Germany and bombs. Like a battle cruiser overwhelming each enemy destroyer in turn by the weight of gun power, Elaine silenced the opposition. One by one they either gave up the argument or got out at stations on the way. The train emptied a good deal, we got seats, and at last only the fat man in the ragged pullover, sitting opposite us and firing occasional shots across the carriage, was left of our opponents. When at last we got out he gathered strength for one last fusillade, in which I caught the words "*cochon*" and "*la vache.*" Elaine did not reply, and as we got out of the carriage I saw him settle back and close his eyes, happy no doubt at having the last word. Outside the station I said, "What was all that about?"

"They said we shouldn't have brought in the cases."

"Yes, but what was all that stuff about Germany?"

"It was the way the Germans behaved during the war, they said. I told them not to be such fools, we'd been their allies. Then they said we'd bombed them. Idiots." There were bright spots on her cheeks. "You weren't much help, for all your Wainwright education."

"French isn't my strong subject," I said with dignity.

"What is?"

I was carrying both the cases and now I dumped them on the pavement. "I wanted to find a hotel straight away, or at least check these bloody things in at the station. It's not my fault we're landed with them, and we're not going to be landed any longer." Some masterful gesture was needed, and luckily at this moment I caught sight of a cab, hailed it, and told the man to take us to the Hôtel Oeil d'Or.

Inside the cab she said, "I didn't mean—it's all right for you, you don't have to worry about money, but I've come over here to try and find out about my uncle, not to gawp at Paris."

"I don't know why you think I'm rich. I've used up my allowance to come here."

"And won't there be more where that came from?" I had no answer to this. "I don't know why you took a taxi, we're not going to have any too much money."

"We're getting rid of these cases. We're staying at the Oeil d'Or."

"Supposing it's expensive?"

"Do you think that's likely, after the other place?"

The Hôtel Oeil d'Or, however, did not at all resemble the Hôtel les deux Pigeons. The rue Mallarmé was shabby but quiet. The hotel was shabby too, but bright and clean. It had also, mercifully, a receptionist who spoke good English. Rooms with breakfast were a hundred francs a night each, not much more than fifteen shillings. They were small but clean, and they had washbasins. Both rooms had views across neighbouring roofs. I raised my eyebrows at Elaine, and she nodded. The two cases were deposited at last—as I put them down I wondered why I had become so exasperated about them, for they were not very heavy—and we went down to sign the register. I said to the receptionist, "We were recommended to come here by a friend of mine. His name is Stiver."

He repeated it, and I repeated it back to him. He shook his head.

"But he stayed here." A thought occurred to me. "It may have been before you came."

He was a small man with a large nose, a wide mouth, and thin hair plastered down and carefully combed to hide the bald patches. He almost visibly swelled at my words. "Monsieur, I am the proprietor. My name is Pasquin."

I was disconcerted. Elaine said, "That's odd, Monsieur Pasquin, because our friend mentioned you. He came over to England for a few days and now he's back in Paris. We'd been hoping to find him here." Pasquin was shaking his head. Elaine suggested that I should describe our friend, and as I did so Pasquin began to smile. His smile became a broad beam of pleasure. I broke off. "You know him?"

"Of course, but why do you call him Stiver? It is Monsieur Blackney. Come along. I show you." He took us into a small sitting-room and began to look through the drawers of a battered desk, muttering to himself as he did so. He was looking through photographs, and at last found the one he wanted. I picked it up. The photograph showed two men standing outside the hotel. One of them was Pasquin, and the other was the man who had called himself David Wainwright.

I looked up to see Monsieur Pasquin unlocking with a key a small corner cupboard. He produced from it three small glasses and a bottle of Armagnac, poured tots carefully into each of the glasses, and ceremoniously handed them to us. We raised them and drank. The brandy ran down inside me like a pleasant river—no, hardly a river, a vein—of fire. Suddenly Pasquin's wide smile was changed to a frown. He had a mobile, changeable face. "But why am I drinking? He owes me money, Percy."

"Percy. Did he call himself that?" Elaine said. Something stirred in my memory and then faded.

"I thought he was a friend," Pasquin said solemnly, and then corrected himself. "I still think of him as a friend, he is my friend."

"You don't know where he might be now?"

"If he were in Paris he would come to see his friend Pierre Pasquin. Or would he come?" Pasquin shrugged, a man who had been much and often deceived. He needed no invitation to talk and we sat in his little sitting-room drinking Armagnac and listening to a story which, while it told us more about David, didn't make very much sense.

Blackney had come to the Hôtel Oeil d'Or some fifteen months earlier, had taken a room for a fortnight, and had stayed on. Pasquin had been in the Resistance, admired the English, and got on well with Blackney from the start. As the little man talked and told us something of his own history, it seemed to me that the visiting Englishman fulfilled some romantic dreams of his own. When the war ended he and his wife had bought the hotel and he had settled down to the routine of peacetime life. They had no children and Madame Pasquin, whom we met a little later, was a large rock-like woman with legs like tree trunks and the arms of a miner. She was, Pasquin conveyed to us, an earthbound practical creature, concerned with the price of vegetables and meat, the iniquities of the maids, the problem of making a living. Blackney must have represented for the little man the dream life that he had hoped might await him at the end of the war. He was unmarried, he had no permanent job, he worked sometimes teaching English to French families, in the summer as a courier for travel firms showing visitors around Paris, occasionally for a short time as a night watchman at some big store. He was often hard up but he was free, or at least that was the way it seemed to Pierre Pasquin. I asked whether they had talked much about the past.

"About the war a little, yes, not very much. Percy was a flyer, in a bomber." He brooded. "He had many missions over Germany, then he was shot down and the Germans caught him."

This fitted in with David. "And then?"

"I do not know. They sent him to a camp. He did not like

to talk about that. There were marks on his body, I saw them once. It was not a thing to talk about. Percy was gay, you understand, he did not talk of such things. Then sometimes he was sad." He hesitated.

"We know he took drugs," I said.

He shook his head. "That was bad, very bad. I spoke to him often, but no good. He said to me he liked them, had to have them. Once he said, 'I am dead, Pierre, and this brings me to life again'."

"He never talked at all about his family in England?"

He shook his head. The recital seemed to have made him gloomy. He was in the act of pouring more Armagnac when the door opened and a woman immediately recognisable as Madame Pasquin appeared. She addressed her husband at length, in a manner plainly uncomplimentary and connected with the Armagnac. When he offered to pour her a glass she brushed away the suggestion with one sweep of her brawny arm. He introduced us in a resigned manner. "English. Friends of Percy Blackney. They are staying here."

She began to upbraid him again. He stopped her. In a way he was absurd, yet there was something dignified about him. "Please speak in English."

His wife looked from him to us with an expression on her slab-like face that was evidently not friendly. She managed to summon four words of English and then turned on her heel, banging the door furiously behind her. The words were, "*I 'ope they pay.*"

Pasquin handed us the glasses of Armagnac. His hand trembled a little. Elaine said, with what was for her surprising gentleness, "Did he owe you much money?"

"Money, what does it matter? We were friends. He told me that he would be rich, he would pay me back."

"When did he say that? Just before he was leaving you?"

"Before? Oh, yes, before. When he had the lessons."

"Lessons? What sort of lessons?"

But this proved hard to establish, partly because Pasquin was himself not quite sure, partly because of the language problem. They were lessons "*en comportement*," that was the nearest we could get to it, and Blackney had seemed to regard them rather as a joke. It seemed that we were approaching the heart of the matter, but who had given Blackney these lessons in comportment or deportment, where were they conducted? Pasquin didn't know. In his time at the Hôtel Oeil d'Or Blackney had had very few visitors, and there seemed to be nobody that we knew among them. Women? No, there had been no women, and the little man did not seem inclined to elaborate upon this point. I described Ulfheim, but Pasquin had not seen him. Could he remember any visitors at all? There had been a young man named Maurice Fallon who had come often at one time, and it seemed that Pasquin had not approved of him. It was during the period of the lessons, which had lasted for several weeks, that Blackney had talked about getting a lot of money, and Pasquin had been pleased for his friend. And then in April Blackney had disappeared. One morning he was there, he did not return all day, and when late in the evening Madame Pasquin had gone up to his room to see if he was ill, she found the room stripped of his few belongings. He had evidently packed the things in his suitcase and then walked out. He had left owing a bill, and perhaps he had borrowed money from the little man as well. Pasquin did not say.

We were still asking questions when an angry bellow could be heard. "Pierre. Pierre." Pasquin looked at us, went to the cupboard and locked it carefully, and picked up the glasses. "You will excuse me. That is Madame Pasquin."

We excused him. When we were all out of the sitting-room he disappeared down stairs that obviously led to the kitchen. Elaine put a hand on my arm. "Look in the register. It might tell us something, where he came from perhaps."

The register, a big red book, was on the desk, and Elaine looked at it while I kept watch. I heard her turning the pages, and then there was an exclamation. She was laughing. She pointed to an entry. I read: "P Blakeney." His nationality was given as British, the place of residence was left blank. The writing was straggly, very much like what I remembered of the letter Lady W had shown me. I could not understand why Elaine was laughing.

"Don't you see? It's not Blackney, it's Blakeney. And his name's Percy. Percy Blakeney, the Scarlet Pimpernel. A joke."

It seemed to me that there was something wrong about that, although I could not be sure what it was. Later I sat on the bed in her room, and we talked about what we had learned. Elaine ticked off points on her fingers. She stood against the window in the fading light, and her neat delicate profile reminded me of a figure in one of the wall tapestries in my bedroom, a young girl who held in her hand some kind of jug, and gravely faced her equally youthful lover. It was the first time I had thought about her, or about any girl, in that way. There was nothing obviously sexual in the thought, but I was conscious that I should like to hold and kiss her.

"First, we know that Percy Blakeney as he called himself came here in April of last year. He did odd jobs that paid for his wants and for his drugs, perhaps he sold drugs himself. About January he began taking these lessons. Obviously he was being taught what to say when the time came for him to pose as David Wainwright, agreed?"

"Yes, I suppose so." She turned towards me full face. She was frowning.

"When was Lady Wainwright taken ill?"

"She's been ill since last November, but nobody knew how serious it was until a few weeks ago."

"Last November. That's when he started the plan."

"Who?"

"The man who gave Blakeney the lessons. Then in April Blakeney leaves here, goes to the awful Hôtel les deux Pigeons under another name. I think the object of that was to cover his tracks a bit, agreed? Meanwhile the lessons go on. If some member of the family comes over, there he is in a hotel where nobody has known him for long. I suppose Stiver was chosen as another joke, I haven't got a stiver, that kind of thing. The lessons go on, they get news that Lady Wainwright is very ill and may die, and the plan is put into operation. What do you think of that?"

"I dare say it's true as far as it goes, but the important thing if you're right is, who's behind Blakeney?"

"Then Blakeney does something wrong, Thorne realises he's a fake, he has to kill Thorne. He gets cold feet and comes back here. But where is he?" She was still frowning. "You might say we're at a dead end. I don't see what else we can do."

While we had been talking to Pasquin my vision of Paris had temporarily faded, but now it returned in full force. "We could go to that place Durcet mentioned."

"What place?"

"He gave you a card."

"Oh, that." She felt in her pocket and brought out a grubby card. It said Taverne Maximilien Robespierre, with a telephone number and an address, 59, rue Babeuf, 4e. She said without much enthusiasm that we could go there if I liked.

I was staring at the card. I could not describe my thought

sequence, which was as inconsequential as some of those Sherlock Holmes talked about to Watson, but Robespierre reminded me of Blakeney, Blakeney reminded me of a scene in an old film in which Sir Percy was looking at a miniature preparatory to disguising himself as a French nobleman shown in the miniature who was to be saved from the clutches of the villainous Chauvelin, and the miniature reminded me—but let me make a jump and say that I saw quite clearly before my eyes the photograph that I had held in my hand years ago when Lady W had first talked to me about David. It showed him with the rest of his crew, and by closing my eyes I could see David again in the middle of the group and the others round him, with their names beneath. "Flt.-Sgt. M Billings, Sgt. V J Copp, Flt.-Lieut. D Wainwright, Sgt. R H T Williams, Cpl. J H Crump, Cpl. R Shalson," and then at the end, "Flt.-Sgt. P Blakeney." I opened my eyes to find Elaine staring at me in astonishment. She asked if I was feeling well.

"Yes. I knew there was something, I knew I should remember." I got up and put my arms round her in my excitement. She did not resist, but merely disengaged herself. I sat down again. "I knew I'd heard the name Blakeney before, seen it rather. It was on a photograph of David's air crew. He was one of them, Sergeant P Blakeney. He was on that last flight. As a matter of fact David mentioned him when he was spinning his story to us after he arrived, said Blakeney had been killed with the others.

"Don't you *see*? David was killed, but Blakeney wasn't. The Germans must have taken him and kept him in prison camp. That's how he knew about David in the RAF, it explains all that. The name is real, not a pseudonym. There isn't even anything odd about it, I expect lots of parents named Blakeney call their sons Percy."

"Bloody fools," she said without rancour. "It certainly explains some things."

"It explains a lot. Very likely he picked up that little book of David's poems after the plane crashed, and the wallet too. Or maybe the Germans found them, thought they belonged to him, and Blakeney just accepted it. When he told his story he simply changed the person who was saved from Blakeney to Wainwright and added in the stuff he'd invented about the Russian labour camp. If he found out something about the early days of the Wainwrights he'd be in a good position to come back and pose as David, at least for a little while."

"There are some big holes."

"I don't see any."

"Well, one question is why the Germans didn't say that there was one survivor when the plane was shot down. I mean, these things usually get known, don't they? But obviously the biggest problem is the question of who told him about the early days. He didn't just have superficial knowledge according to you, he knew all about David's childhood and friends. He couldn't just have picked that up."

It was almost dark in the room. I could not see her face. "Yes, that's a problem. But you agree, don't you, that it would be too much of a coincidence that there was a man on that last flight named P Blakeney. It must be the same man."

"Yes, but it doesn't help much. Of course, there's one person who could have told him about the early days of the Wainwrights."

I felt suddenly that I wanted to see her face. I switched on the bedside light which, like so many lights in hotel bedrooms abroad, was dim. She stood by the window, face averted from me, her fingers playing with the acorn on a window blind. "Who do you mean? What person?"

"Why, David himself."

"You mean David's alive?" I couldn't take it in. "But that's crazy. Why didn't he come back himself?"

"Isn't it obvious? He killed my uncle. If he came back himself he was afraid he'd be arrested."

It took a little while for the idea to sink in. Then I said, "But if you're right, what was the point of sending Blakeney? If he was accepted as David, then he'd be arrested too."

"There must have been what you might call an escape clause. Something like this. What David hoped was that everything would go smoothly, Blakeney would be accepted, nobody would make trouble about a case that was nine years old. But suppose the worst happened and the police were going to arrest Blakeney, then he would be able to prove that he wasn't David."

"How?"

"Oh, how do I know? Perhaps he had some birthmark, perhaps he had relations in England who could have identified him."

"Perhaps. It's very theoretical."

"All right, produce a better theory."

That I couldn't do, but I didn't accept any theory that ignored the mysterious Ulfheim and his suggestion that Sullivan's death had had something to do with German agents operating in Kent during the war. I didn't want to argue, however, what I wanted was to get out into the Paris streets again, and in particular to get to the Taverne Maximilien Robespierre.

When we were downstairs again I looked for Pasquin, but found only his mountainous wife. I began to speak to her but Elaine took over from me, and seemed for once to conduct successfully a quite lengthy conversation. Afterwards in the street, I said, "What was all that?"

"She wanted to know whether we would be in to dinner. I said we wouldn't. She's rather melted towards us, seems to have made up her mind that we're innocents abroad. When I told her where we were going she said we must be very careful."

"Why?"

"She said it was a most unpleasant place." Elaine looked at me and burst out laughing. I began to laugh too. "Sorry I was so mean in there."

"Why were you?"

"I'm just mean by nature." We were squeezed together on the narrow pavement by two men going the other way, and our hands touched. She put her hand in mine, and we walked along like that.

Chapter Thirteen

The Taverne

Certain things in one's life stand out vividly, not because they are of importance in themselves, but because they represent so perfectly the quality of one's feelings at the time. Elaine and I walked from our hotel to the Taverne. We did not even think of taking the Métro or a bus, but simply walked along, captured by the magic of the city at night, going in what we knew was roughly the right direction but unconcerned about when, or perhaps even whether, we should finally arrive. We wasted time, but what was time for that evening if not to waste, on the Ile St Louis by walking round the island instead of across it, round by the Quai de Bourbon and the Quai d'Anjou, stopping often to look down into the water or to watch the *bateaux mouches* go by, blazing with light. Often since then I have stood outside a crowded room looking in on people all of whom seemed to know each other, and have felt myself a stranger. This sense of isolation has grown in me with the passing years. But on this evening my happiness was such that, as I looked down at the river boats I felt that they were prisoners, enclosed as they were in their glass cabin, and that the whole world of Paris, of excitement and adventure, belonged to me.

We crossed over to the Right Bank at last, and then lost ourselves among the streets leading off the Bibliothèque de l'Arsenal. We did not ask the way, and hardly spoke to each other. Once Elaine got out her map, but she put it away when I shook my head and we walked on, coming at length to the rue St Antoine, crossing it, going through a wide archway and finding ourselves unexpectedly in the Place des Vosges. I stopped, fascinated by the elegance of the arcades, the gardens in the centre and the identical mansions surrounding three sides of the square. Elaine too was caught by the beauty of it and we walked slowly round. We stopped outside no 6, the Musée Victor Hugo, but of course it was closed—happily enough, for I found it extremely boring on a later visit. I recalled that Gautier had lived next door.

Why do I put down all this? I don't know, except that perhaps it helps to express my state of mental intoxication and to explain the unreality of everything else that happened during the evening. When, quite suddenly, we came upon the Taverne Maximilien Robespierre, I would have been prepared for a welcome inside it from Robespierre himself and the other members of the Revolutionary Committee.

The Taverne was painted black outside. Within there could be seen a glimmer of light. The entrance doors were black with thick obscured glass, and when we pushed them open it was to find ourselves in a square anteroom where everything was red, the tables, a small sofa, the walls, and of course the electric light which cast a dull red glow around. There was a door on our right, and we pushed this open to find ourselves in a long narrow room done in green with small red lights dotted about. These were the glimmers we had seen from outside. Small and large tables topped with green glass were set at irregular intervals. It was possible to see that people were sitting at some of these tables, but their faces were indistinguishable. The general effect was that of being in an aquarium where red lights marked, to put it more fancifully, the more dangerous fish. I stumbled over somebody's foot, and then we found an empty table and sat down. Conversation could be heard around us, continuous as the whispering of crickets. In the stress of surprise Elaine lapsed into American.

"What's it all in aid of? This is a hell of a joint."

Above her a head grinned out at me from the wall, and I saw that at least part of my expectation had been fulfilled. This was the head of Robespierre, lighted from inside, with the handkerchief tied round his face as it had been after his arrest, when part of his jaw was shot away. Looking round I saw that other scenes from the Revolution appeared round the walls. There was Marie Antoinette riding in the tumbrel, Marat in his bath, the trial of Louis XVI. These panels were set into the wall and lighted from inside.

Elaine was just asking whether we should have a drink or leave straight away when a voice said, "Christopher." The word seemed to be so much a part of the general cricket chirring, and it seemed so impossible that anybody in this place would know me, that I ignored it. It was repeated. "Christopher, Christopher Barrington."

Elaine faced the room, I had my back to it, but now I turned to see a number of shadowy figures advancing on me. The foremost one put a hand on my shoulder. It was Betty Urquhart.

"I knew I recognised that head-up look, as though you weren't quite sure where the earth was. Glad you've reached the home of civilisation." Before I knew what was happening she had kissed me firmly on the mouth, adding amiably to Elaine, "Don't worry, doesn't mean anything, I've got a licence to kiss every man under twenty-five. Are you going to introduce me, Chris?"

At another time I would have thought, this can't be happening, but in the green and red light nothing seemed unlikely, and I was murmuring Elaine's name while Betty, in a much louder voice which still seemed to blend with the anonymous buzz around us, was naming her friends, the action painter Max Miners, Norman Beaver, Sally Metz, and a man named Carl whose surname I never discovered. In no time we were all sitting at one table and Betty, with a snap of her fingers, had summoned up service in the form of a young man wearing what seemed to be a green striped apron and a plain green blouse. She was obviously well known here.

"What are we drinking? *Pastis*, of course, except for that bloody barbarian Norman and his Scotch. Chris, you'll drink *pastis*, won't you? And what about you, darling?"

"Beer!" Elaine's voice sounded emphatic.

Betty sat next to me on the banquette that faced the room. "You two are having a ball in Paris, is that right?" She brushed aside my attempt to say that it was not. "Nowhere better, my dear, nowhere better. I could do with some romance myself. You haven't brought my ex along with you, I suppose? Pity. Paris would be just the place to make a man of him, put some lead in his pencil."

Across the table I could hear Max Miners saying to Elaine, "I tell you why I like this place. They say at night all cats are grey, down here they're all red and green. Now I'm black and I'm sensitive about that, you get me, but down here what does it matter?"

The drinks came and I tasted mine. That is another of the things I shall never forget, the taste of the green drink in the green room. I had never tasted it before and from the first sip of that strange mixture, the blend of paregoric with something cold, remote, and in an obscure way sexually stirring and liberating, I knew that this was a drink for me. Something of this must have shown in my face even in the dim light, for Betty said, "You like this snake juice?"

"Snake juice?"

"Didn't you know? The damned stuff's poison, I wish I didn't like it so much."

"David, the man who said he was David, was a fake."

"Of course he was, didn't I say so five minutes after I saw him?"

"I know, but—" I didn't feel I could tell her about Doctor Foster, and indeed that whole scene at Belting seemed at this moment extremely remote. "He's come over here, he ran away from Belting. We're here to look for him."

"Why here?"

"They say he comes to this place." I tried to remember who had said so, but couldn't. It didn't seem to matter.

"Does he? Well, half the riff-raff in Paris get in here at one time or another. What are you going to do with him when you've got him?"

It was a question to which I couldn't think of a reply.

On the other side of me Sally Metz said, "You a poet or a painter?"

I said boldly, "A poet."

"Shake, Chris, so am I." We shook hands. She was a big blonde woman with a face like an intelligent horse and an incongruous curl in the middle of her forehead. "But what do you do about words?"

"How do you mean?"

"They're the hell of writing poetry, I find, the way paint's the trouble for a painter. I mean there they all are, what do you *do* with them? A painter like Max, see, he's got this technique of throwing the stuff at a wall, photographing the effect and taking it from there by tracing the photographs on a canvas and copying it, so it's impersonal. But how do you get poetry impersonal like that? The words mean too much, isn't that right?"

"I can't say it's ever bothered me."

"You're a Georgian then." She turned away to talk to Carl. I found that another drink was in front of me, and began to protest that I must pay.

"Don't be a fool, Chris," Betty said. "I own this place."

I gaped at her. Was she joking? "Didn't you know I was stinking rich? Not stinking actually, just a bit filthy, but I don't mind telling you it's a curse."

"But you said you were trying to be an actress."

"That was a long time ago. I stepped into the stuff with both feet when my father died after the war. Since then I've tried to do something for art, but how do you tell what's real from what's phoney?" I couldn't answer that. "Do you like it here? I had it done by a young man who said he had ideas, and perhaps he had but I don't know. I don't know at all."

"Do you own any other property?" It seemed a ridiculous form of words, and she obviously thought so too.

"I don't own property, Chris, I encourage art. I've got a little gallery here, put on a show of some Russian named Chromik. Everyone told me he was a genius, but we never sold a single painting. And the Seven Arts Coffee House, just round the corner from the People's Art Gallery, I own that too. Bookshop on the ground floor, jazz and coffee bar downstairs. Shall I tell you something bloody awful, Chris? This place here makes money and so does the Seven

Arts. They're commercial enterprises, see, I can't go wrong on those, but when it comes to painters and writers I back losers every time."

"Yes, I see that's a problem."

"I sometimes think the only real thing I ever had was life with Miles."

"Who are those other two men?"

"Carl's a painter, some people say he's good. I'm supposed to be putting on his first one-man show here. Norman Beaver's a playwright, he's taking us to—"

"What about Henrik?" Norman said from the other side of the table. "Got to make a move, Bets."

She turned to face me. Green points of light were reflected in her eyes. "Why don't you two come?"

"Come where?"

"Some Ibsen play Norman's mad about, says it's a model for modern verse drama or something. A friend of his is directing it, Paul Delmain. We can manage another couple of seats, can't we, Norman?"

"I've got pull enough for that, Bets. I don't imagine it will be a full house anyway."

"I'd love to come." My voice sounded loud in my own ears. I realised that I'd forgotten to ask Elaine. "We'd love it, wouldn't we?"

"Yes." The monosyllable was not encouraging.

We went out in a noisy group. As we moved out of the dim green room into the equally dim red entrance, two figures walked out of this red anteroom into the street. Half a minute passed by the time Betty had got her coat and we were outside in the rue Babeuf, and during that half-minute I tried to remember why I had noticed the figures. That is putting it too precisely, for under the influence of *pastis* one does not "try to remember" anything, although I did not know this at the time. *Pastis* is like no other intoxicant that I have tasted, in that it actually clears the mind so that one's thought processes are not blunted but sharpened, yet at the same time it makes the communication of one's wholly logical thoughts and arguments extremely difficult. A neglected poet has well expressed the effect of drinking it:

> *Gently I wave the visible world away.*
> *A roar is in my ears, afar yet near,*
> *Far off yet near a voice is in my ear.*
> *And is the voice my own? The words I say*
> *Fall faintly, like a dream, across the day.*

If my senses had not been sharpened by those two glasses of *pastis* very likely I should not have seen anything familiar about the two figures who left the Taverne before us, but if I had by chance noticed them then I might have run after them but for the deadly influence of the green drink. Instead I said calmly, almost indifferently, as the two figures appeared briefly under a street lamp before turning into the street that led to the Place des Vosges, "There go David and Ulfheim."

Betty, who was talking earnestly to Max Miners, said, "What did you say, Chris?" The rest of them except for Elaine took no notice. Why should they have done? Elaine was standing beside me. She gripped my arm. "Where?"

I pointed, but there was now nobody to be seen. "They were in the Taverne. They left just before us."

She ran up the street. I stood and watched her. When she came back she said, "Nothing."

"They've gone. I didn't make a mistake."

"Then why didn't—" She began in exasperation, and stopped. "Do you feel all right?"

"Perfectly."

"You're not fit to be out on your own. That's the only reason I'm coming," she said savagely.

Somehow the seven of us crowded into the little red car, three in front and four behind. I was wedged between Elaine and Sally Metz, wedged in such a manner that none of us was really sitting down, yet all had a share of the limited seating space. Norman Beaver sat on Sally's knees, and he kept up a running flow of comment on what we were going to see, or perhaps it would be more accurate to say a flow of comment about its relation to his own work.

"They say verse drama's out, isn't that so, but that's because they're looking for the wrong sort of verse drama, don't you see?"

This was at a time when *The Lady's Not For Burning* had recently been produced successfully and I interjected, "Fry." The word was misunderstood.

"Fry, you're right, let 'em fry, or stew in their own Eliot-juice if you like. It's all guff, isn't it, all verse and no drama, but Ibsen is something else again. With him it's the way it is with Shakespeare, drama first every time, and that's the way it is with me too in *Marco Polo Shoots the Moon*."

"I haven't heard of that," Elaine said.

"How would you, when it hasn't been produced? It takes eight hours to play, they say I've got to cut it. What the hell, I told them, Shaw's *Methuselah* took longer, and you know what they said to me? They said 'You're not Methuselah'." He guffawed. It occurred to me that another reply would have been "You're not Shaw," but I did not say so.

The Secte, which was the name of the theatre, was in Montmartre, off the Place Pigalle, and it was of a kind new to me at that time, although I have visited a good many similar theatres since then. It was in a large basement room, and there were perhaps a hundred seats, some of them very close to the small stage. Norman bustled about as soon as he got inside, talking to a crop-headed narrow-waisted young man who wore tight trousers. He came back and announced triumphantly that the seats were okay, although since the theatre was only half-full this was not surprising. We had been in our seats only a couple of minutes when the play began.

I had never heard then of *Love's Comedy*, or *Comédie d'Amour* as the programme naturally had it, and my ignorance was excusable, for I doubt if many even of the devoutest Ibsenites have seen it performed. It was written in 1862 but not actually performed, even in Norway, for another decade. The last English performance took place in 1909, and I should think it unlikely that the play had ever before been staged in Paris. *Love's Comedy* presents one of the essential Ibsenite dramas or conflicts, between the forces of art and society. Falk, a young poet, is in love with Svanhild, who shares his contempt for the petty everyday world around them. The conflict is repeated in the lives of everybody else in the play—a student, a clergyman, a clerk—they are all married or intending to marry, and with marriage abandoning the poetic pretensions which they had at one time. In the end Falk and Svanhild agree to part in the interests of Falk's genius, precisely because they do love each other. She tears off his ring, throws it into a fjord, and cries:

> *My task is done!*
> *Now I have filled thy soul with song and sun.*
> *Forth! Now thou soarest on triumphant wings.*
> *Forth! Now thy Svanhild is the swan that sings!*
> *To the abysmal ooze of ocean bed*
> *Descend, my dream—I fling thee in its stead.*

Whether or not *Love's Comedy* had a revolutionary effect on verse drama, whether indeed it influenced *Marco Polo Shoots the Moon*, I shall never know. I can't even be sure whether we saw a well-acted version of it, although there seemed to me to be a good deal more declamation and gesticulation than I care for on the stage. At some time during the first act I was nagged by a feeling that something in the play was of special significance for me, and the attempt to discover this significance became at last so overwhelming that I could hardly sit in my seat. Something about *Love's Comedy* held a message for me, and I did not know what it was.

Dissatisfaction was expressed by others, for different reasons. "Shall we go?" Betty asked after the second act. "I'm hungry."

Norman was shocked. "We ought to stay, Bets, or Paul's going to be upset. You know how temperamental he is. I said he should join us afterwards, is that all right?"

"Yes, but I don't know if I can last out. I thought you said Paul was a genius."

Max Miners said, "Paul's one hell of a nice feller. I don't care whether he's a genius as a director or not, or what sort of friends he's got. He's a nice feller."

"Who's arguing about it? He was just sold to me as a genius, that's all."

It seemed strange to me that they should talk about the director rather than the play, but I have learned since then that some people interested in the theatre always do that. I asked Sally Metz what she thought. I might have guessed.

"I don't know, I just don't know. For me there are too many words and they're not always in the right order."

That was a criticism sufficiently sibylline to be safe, but I suppose the safest attitude of all was that of Carl, who didn't speak a word the whole evening that I heard. Elaine was silent too, and I was struck by the difference between her usual aggressiveness and her defensive attitude in the presence of these not very intimidating people. It seemed to me that she was not enjoying herself as I was. I asked her during this interval whether she wanted to go.

"Do *you* want to go?"

The serenity induced by the *pastis* combined with the sense that the play contained a message for me inspired my answer. "No, I'm very happy."

"It's a good thing somebody's happy. I suppose this is all really subtle detective work, and you're on the verge of making some marvellous discovery."

She was perfectly right.

Chapter Fourteen

After the Theatre

The Taverne Maximilien Robespierre served food late in the evening, and made some concessions to patrons when it did so. The anteroom was still blood red, but the lighting in the long inner room had been changed. It was now of some mysterious golden shade that made men look bronzed and healthy, while contriving to leave women still palely elegant. One end of the room was reserved for those who drank and played chess, and the other was set with check cloths for those who wanted to eat. A long table had been kept for us, and Betty led the way to it. A man wearing a chef's hat popped his head out of a cubbyhole beside our table and she said that we would have the usual. To us, when his head had popped back again, she said, "There's a menu as long as your arm, but steak *au poivre* is the only thing he can cook well, that and bacon and eggs. And he was sold to me as a bloody genius too."

She must have ordered more drinks, because I found in front of me a glass containing the now familiar thick green liquid. Water dripped slowly into it through a container, clouding the liquid and subtly changing its colour. I watched the process in fascination, then held up my hand and the dripper was taken away. I sipped the drink, looked up, and saw a man weaving a way through the tables towards us, rather uncertainly. It was Uncle Miles.

It says much for the calmness induced by *pastis* that I accepted his presence there as something perfectly natural, and merely raised a hand in welcome. Betty, however, got up and embraced him. Uncle Miles responded with a peck at her cheek.

"You look just the same," she cried. "Except for the hair. But I like it, do you know I think it gives you real distinction?"

Uncle Miles rubbed his hands together in anticipation of a little joke. "You always did say I was bad-tempered, didn't you, couldn't keep my hair on."

Betty ignored this. She put an arm round him. "This is my ex, and I want to tell you all he's the sweetest man I ever lived with. You just sit down and tell me what you're doing in Paris, and have a drink."

Uncle Miles giggled. "I've already had two or three. But I won't say no. First, though, I must have a word with our mutual friend."

"Chris? I don't mind telling you, Chris is a marvellous boy. He's just sat through the most bloody boring play without falling asleep. You know his friend Elinor, don't you?"

Elaine had put on her spectacles. "Elaine. Elaine Sullivan."

"We met one day in Folkestone." Uncle Miles turned to me. "I expect you wonder how I come to be here, but it's really terribly simple. You shouldn't have gone off like that."

"You got my note?"

"Yes, and you left that bit of paper with the address of the Hôtel Oeil d'Or, so we guessed you'd be staying there.

When I called there M. Pasquin said you'd told his wife you were coming here. So here I am."

There was a sudden pop beside my ear. Glasses were being filled with champagne. "It's not every day you meet up with an ex," Betty said.

"I say, champers." Uncle Miles swallowed the contents of his glass at a gulp.

I pushed my glass across to him and ignored Elaine's basilisk glare across the table. "Here, have mine. I shall have more snake juice."

The green liquid was poured, the dripper began its work. "I don't see why you've come," I said, and added in case this sounded discourteous, "Although I'm pleased to see you."

The bubbles had got up Uncle Miles' nose. He wrinkled it. "We don't know how to tell Mamma. The news about David, I mean. I've come to bring you back."

To this I found no reply. Just then the steaks arrived, and we began to eat them. More champagne was opened. Uncle Miles was in ecstasies.

"Isn't this a mistake, with red-blooded meat? Never mind, it's a treat anyway." He raised his glass to Betty, who clinked glasses with him. Max Miners protested that he wanted burgundy.

"Oh, you do," Betty said. "You don't like the champagne."

Max flapped a pinky-black hand. "It's just not right. Nobody with a palate could drink it with steak."

"They couldn't?" Betty had spoken calmly, but her voice was suddenly raised to a shriek. "So perhaps you'd just like to get yourself out of here. You're abusing my hospitality."

"If that's what you want. If I go I don't come back, you know that. You think you can insult a man just because of the colour of his skin, but you'll find you're wrong. There's a day coming—"

Betty used a quadriliteral that I had never heard a woman use before. At another time I might have been shocked but on this particular evening it seemed part of the whole dreamlike situation. The response from Max Miners was a flood of abuse which I suppose I had better not set down. Uncle Miles stood up. He was a head shorter than Max, and he held on to the back of his chair for support, but his voice was deep as a gong.

"Now, sir, just remember that you're speaking to a lady." The painter goggled at him, and then walked away. Uncle Miles sat down again, rather shakily. Betty was wiping her eyes. "Miles, darling, you'll be the death of me, I haven't been called a lady for years. Still, that's one genius got rid of. Oh, my God, here comes another."

Weaving through the crowd in the Taverne (it was now almost full, and there was a considerable hubbub of conversation) came the crop-headed young man from the theatre. Behind him glided another young man, of an elegant willowy handsomeness. He wore a long gold earring in one ear and a large emerald ring on one hand.

"Paul, what you did was terrific, but I've got to say it, you were let down by your actors," Norman Beaver said. Paul raised his eyebrows, not at all disconcerted by the criticism, which was voiced as though it were praise. "I think you know everybody, Betty of course, Sally and Carl, you know Betty's putting on a show of his stuff. And—"

"Chris Barrington and his friend Elinor," Betty said. "And my old man, my ex, come all the way over here to see me. I don't know about the others, Paul, but I thought your old Ibsen was lousy."

"You're always frank," Paul spoke without enthusiasm. "Paul Delmain. Maurice Fallon."

They sat down, Delmain next to Norman Beaver, his companion beside me. Elaine leaned across the table. It was the first time she had addressed me since we returned to the Taverne, and I leaned over towards her, so that we must have presented the appearance of puppets simultaneously jerked together.

"Did you hear that?"

"What?"

"His name, Maurice Fallon. Pasquin told us."

I remembered then, perfectly. I turned to the young man. "I think you know a friend of mine."

His eyes were a bright shallow blue. "What?"

"Blakeney. Percy Blakeney."

Uncle Miles beat on the table with a spoon and sang:

> *"Champers with steak, champers with steak,*
> *That's a discovery all of us make."*

Fallon gesticulated. The light caught the emerald on his hand. He said in heavily accented English, "What are you trying to do?"

"Trying to find him, that's all."

"Then you better look in the right place."

"He was a friend of yours, wasn't he?"

"A friend." His laughter was shrill. Paul Delmain looked anxiously at us.

"He's back in Paris now. I thought he might have been in touch with you."

"With me. Why should that be?"

"You used to see a lot of him, so I was told. I thought he was a friend of yours."

"Not of mine. Why should I care for him?" He brought his face close to mine. "He is taking perhaps some more *lessons*. He is being taught some more *magic*."

"I don't know what you mean."

Delmain had been talking to Norman Beaver. Now he broke off to address Fallon rapidly in French. The sense of it seemed to be that Fallon shouldn't get upset. What he said had no effect. Fallon spat at me, not intentionally I am sure, but I could feel the spittle on my face. "You should look for him in the rue Peter Paul, he will be learning more magic." I had no idea what he meant. The expression on his face changed to one of contempt. "But he will not be interested."

"Why not?"

He drew back a little, looked over as much as he could see of me with a gaze that was like a rake of claws, and repeated scornfully, "Oh no, I do not think he will be interested."

The ring in his ear swung a little, and I followed its movement. Delmain was on his feet. Fallon flung down his napkin and got up too. Delmain inclined his cropped head stiffly.

"Norman. Betty. We are going."

I knew I had said something wrong, but couldn't be sure what it was. It seemed to me that there must be something more to be learned from Fallon. "I'm sorry," I said. "Don't go."

They might as well not have heard the words, and perhaps they didn't. "Good riddance," Betty said. "Another genius gone. I've had geniuses."

"What did you say to upset Paul's boy friend so much," Norman Beaver asked me.

"Boy friend?"

"What did you think?"

The words came to me like a revelation, the whole evening had been a revelation, but what had it revealed? I understood only that action was vital, and urgent. "We must act."

"I was an actor once," Uncle Miles said.

I tried to stand up and discovered one of the other qualities of *pastis*, that while increasing the acuity of the mind it has a most disconcerting effect upon the legs. My legs felt as though they were not there, and it was certainly impossible for me to stand upon them. I sat down again, put my hands on my legs to make certain that they existed, and repeated what I had said. Elaine was looking at me oddly. Betty asked if I was all right, and I was delighted to hear the clarity with which I answered her.

Immediately afterwards I felt my trunk moving sideways. The sensation was a strange one, for I had the impression that I was watching this from outside and that I actually saw my body's slow keeling over on to the table, although of course this cannot really have been the case. My left elbow knocked over some glasses, and then the whole top part of my body rested on the table. I heard voices, but they seemed to come from far away. The need for action receded and I was conscious only of serenity, abiding peace.

Chapter Fifteen

The Magician

I opened my eyes and shut them again instantly. Outside there was a harsh intolerable light that screwed up the eyeballs. With the lids shut things were better. Or were they? My head felt as if it were being struck regular blows with a hammer and when I raised it a little, still with closed eyes, I felt an atrocious pain in the neck. Had I been involved in an accident and landed in hospital? Cautiously I opened my eyes again, and with even greater caution lifted my head. I was in bed, in my room at the Hôtel Oeil d'Or, and I was wearing pyjamas. The discovery, although reassuring in a way, was too much for me. I sank back on to the pillows and groaned.

A couple of minutes later I made a daring move. I raised my whole body, swung my legs out of bed, and put my feet to the floor. The hammers pounded on my head, and my mouth felt as if a bonfire had been lighted in it and the remains were still smouldering. I stood up with the help of a bedpost, and measured the distance from bed to washbasin. Three strides. I felt the Ancient Mariner's need for water. If water could be sprayed inside my mouth and splashed over my head I felt that I might live, but could I reach the washbasin without falling? Relinquishing the bedpost I flung myself forward. I did not fall, but caught my head a nasty crack against a glass shelf just above the basin. I was pouring water into and over myself when the door opened. Elaine stood there, in light blue blouse and dark blue skirt, looking extremely bright and fresh.

She was not sympathetic. "I thought you were dead, but I see you've woken. It's ten o'clock." I groaned, and stretched out a hand for help to return to bed. "What do you think you're doing?"

"Back to bed."

"Nonsense. We've got things to do."

I said feebly, "What things?"

"Last night you kept saying we must go to some street or other – the rue Peter Paul. I don't know why."

I managed to reach the bedpost again, and sat down shakily. "What happened last night?"

"You passed out. Beaver and that poetess and I brought you back here. Beaver and Pasquin put you to bed."

"Where was Uncle Miles?"

Her smile was grim. "He passed out too, five minutes after you. Betty Urquhart took him home. Do you think she's attractive?"

The hammer thudded so loudly I hardly knew what I was saying. "Yes, I suppose so."

"More than I am? Perhaps you don't think I'm attractive at all."

I felt unable to cope with this. "Don't be silly."

It was obvious that I had said the wrong thing. "You certainly made a pretty fair fool of yourself last night. Surely you realised that young man was queer."

"Fallon, you mean."

"Who else? Obviously he was a friend of Blakeney's and then the magic man, whoever he is, replaced Fallon, and Fallon was jealous. He thought you were another rival. But I suppose you were too tight to grasp any of it. The Wainwrights certainly can't carry their liquor."

"I wasn't tight. I remember everything perfectly." And as I said it, I did remember everything, the play, the conversation with Fallon, and the conclusions I had drawn. But there was something else, something Elaine had said this morning. "What was it you said?"

"What are you talking about?"

"When you came in here you said something."

She repeated it, as if she were speaking to a child. "I said that I thought you were dead, but I saw you'd woken up."

"Of course," I said. "Ulfheim."

I sank back on the bed. Now I held all the threads in my hands. I knew why Blakeney had been sent over to England, why Arbuthnot had spoken as he had, who had killed Sullivan and Thorne.

"Come *on*," Elaine said. "Get up."

"Just a minute. The programme."

"What programme?"

"The play. *Comédie d'Amour*. Have you got it?"

She looked at me as if she thought I were mad, then without a word went out of the room and came back with a copy of the programme, which she thrust at me. I pointed at the names of the characters with a shaky finger, and picked out two: "*Styver, a clerk*", "*Straamand, a clergyman.*"

"Well?"

"I knew while I was watching the play that there was something I ought to understand about it. The man who called himself Wainwright took the name of Stiver in Paris, and do you know what an anglicisation of Straamand is? It's Strawman. If you remember, Ulfheim said we could call him Strawman, a clergyman."

She put on her spectacles as though they might enable her to see through this fog. "What then?"

"The two names came from this play, *Comédie d'Amour*."

"And how does that help?"

"Ulfheim, too. I remembered when you said you thought I was dead, but I'd woken up. Ulfheim is a character in Ibsen's last play. Do you know what it's called? *When We Dead Awaken*."

"I still don't understand."

"No, I suppose you need a special sense of humour to understand why that's funny." I sighed and gathered myself together. "Come on, then, there's no time to lose."

She began to laugh. "Speaking of sense of humour, you've no idea how funny you looked in that place, falling sideways like a statue."

"I'm sure. If you'll go out, I'll get dressed."

She walked over and stood at the window, with her back to me. "I don't want you falling asleep again. I won't look."

"Thanks."

"You do think I'm as attractive as that woman, don't you?"

"Betty? I told you not to be silly. She's old."

As I was shakily putting on my trousers she said, still with her back to me, "I'll tell you something else that happened last night. After you'd been put to bed you got up again and came into my room."

"What happened?"

"Don't you remember?"

"Well—"

"Then you'll never find out, will you?" And in fact I never did.

Ten minutes later I was dressed and descending the stairs, feeling still distinctly shaky. As we passed Pasquin's sitting-room the little man popped out, drew us aside, and patted me on the shoulder.

"How are you? Fairly rotten, I expect."

"Yes."

"But you had fun, you had a good time?"

"It was a good time while it lasted."

Pasquin had unlocked the drink cupboard, and I was afraid that he was going to offer us Armagnac, which I should have had to refuse. But when he turned he was holding a glass containing a pinky-white liquid. "For you." I looked at it doubtfully. "You know what Percy used to say, 'This is the pick-me-up that never lets you down.' That is a joke."

"Yes." I held the glass in my hand, then raised it to my lips and determinedly drained it. The result was touch and go. My stomach seemed to revolt against it, then revolt was succeeded by acceptance and a grateful warmth spread through me. Pasquin watched, then patted my shoulder again. "Now you are better."

"Much better."

"You go and find Percy now, and when you find him you bring him back here."

I said we would. But we never brought Percy back to Pierre Pasquin.

The sunlight outside made me doubtful of my recovery, and my condition was not improved by the sight of Uncle Miles on the pavement. He looked distinctly greenish, but had the air of a man prepared to do his duty. He was accompanied by Betty, her hair brassy as ever. She was wearing what looked like the identical paint-stained trousers that she had on when I first saw her.

"I've come to take you back," Uncle Miles said firmly, although with a restraint that suggested he might give way to sickness at any moment.

With equal firmness I said, "No."

He put his hand to his head. "Christopher, please. I am really not up to argument this morning."

"Then come on." A taxi was passing. When we were all inside I said, "This won't take long. At least, I hope not."

"Where are we going?"

"To the rue Peter Paul."

"I don't think I can bear it." Uncle Miles was referring to the motion of the taxi, which was erratic. He put a hand on his stomach.

Betty patted his knee. "You can't believe what a relief it is not to be with a genius who's got a stomach made of brass."

"What I don't see," Elaine said, for her almost hesitantly, "is, do you know what Fallon meant when he talked about a magician?"

"Yes."

"Was it some sort of code?"

"No. He was talking about a magician."

"Please." Uncle Miles was still holding his stomach. "I am not up to smart talk this morning, I am just not up to it. Please."

"Do you expect to find him with Blakeney?" Elaine asked.

"I don't know. But Blakeney will have gone to him, I know that."

As soon as we stepped out of the taxi we saw the ambulance. It had stopped outside a house half-way down the street, and we joined the dozen people clustered around. I told Elaine to ask them why they were there, but this proved unnecessary. They were bringing the body out of one of the mean, picturesque houses as we came up to it. The blanket covering it slipped aside as they were lifting it into the ambulance, and I saw the face of the man who had called himself David Wainwright. Uncle Miles saw it too, gasped, and turned away. The dead man's face was worn, but he looked more peaceful than I had seen him look in life. There was a neat hole almost in the middle of his forehead. Perhaps it is true that one becomes quickly habituated to death, for I felt none of the disgust and horror that had moved me when I saw Thorne's body, nothing but a sense of pity. Policemen began to push back the onlookers. Elaine looked at me questioningly.

"Ask where the body was discovered. And try to find out where the magician is, Monsieur Magique. Tell them you're a reporter. After all, it's the truth."

Betty looked at me with mock-admiration. "You are masterful."

Elaine began talking to a slatternly woman standing in a doorway. Soon there was a group of half a dozen people, all talking at once. A few minutes later she came back.

"He was found this morning in the hall of that house, by the concierge. They seem to think he was killed last night."

"And Monsieur Magique?"

"He lives in the house. He has a puppet show which he does twice a day. It's somewhere in the Luxembourg Gardens."

I ran to the end of the street, and we took another taxi. It put us down in the rue de Vaugirard, by the gate on the east side of the Palais du Luxembourg. As we entered the gardens I stood staring at the palace.

"You won't find anybody giving puppet shows there," Elaine said.

But I was checked, overwhelmed by the associations the palace must have for anybody with my kind of romantic feeling for French revolutionary history. In this mock palazzo Tom Paine had been imprisoned when he voted against the execution of the King, here Hebert, Danton and Camille Desmoulins had been kept before their trial, here David had drawn his first sketch for the painting of the Sabine women – I could go on, but at some cost to the pace of my narrative. Ahead of us stretched a terrace and a long avenue lined with statues, to our left was the traffic of the Boulevard St Michael, to our right were dusty lawns. Uncle Miles pointed with a shaking hand in this direction and said that he remembered a puppet theatre over there. We crossed these lawns on which children played, as they do in England, but with a polite, shy formality that you will not find here. We came to tennis courts where young men lazily knocked a ball over a net, a café, and the theatre of Uncle Miles' recollection, but this was a long-established marionette theatre, and it made no mention of Monsieur Magique. We had crossed almost the whole gardens from east to west when we found it. In the part of the gardens opposite the rue Auguste Comte there stood a kind of marquee. A dusty signpost pointed to it: "Monsieur Magique."

There was a small cubbyhole saying that the price of admission was Fr. 15, but nobody was there to take money. We pushed open a flap like the flap of a tent, and went inside. Monsieur Magique was on the stage.

In a sense the effect was one of anti-climax. The audience was composed of children and their parents, and the entertainment, or the last few minutes of it that we saw, was in the plane of that provided by a moderately talented conjurer. To be fair, I learned afterwards that the early part of the show was more original, containing puppet variants of fairy tales like "The Sleeping Beauty" and "The Little Match Girl." But while we were there Monsieur Magique, dressed as a pierrot, called children up to him and drew eggs from their noses, discovered a moth-eaten rabbit beneath a boy's pullover, changed water into fizzy lemonade.

"I don't see why the hell you've brought us here," Betty said in a loud voice. Then she stopped. Something, it must have been one of the conjurer's movements or gestures, had caught her attention. She sat staring at the stage. I whispered, "Look at Miles," to Elaine. He was sitting on the other side of Betty, with his mouth turned down, rubbing his eyes with his knuckles as though he were a small boy. He glanced once at me, shook his head unbelievingly, and went on staring at the figure on the stage.

That Monsieur Magique had heard Betty's words was made evident only by the slight jerk of his head. Just for a moment he seemed to look over the heads of the children to us at the back of the tent. But he went on to perform what was evidently the main feature of the show, as he put a small boy into a cabinet, made him disappear, and brought him back again to the accompaniment of a magnesium flash. This act was obviously familiar to a considerable portion of the audience, and was a tremendous success. Monsieur Magique bowed and disappeared behind a curtain. The children filed out happily, asking their mothers how it had been done. Within a couple of minutes we were left alone under the canvas, dusty grass beneath our feet. Betty and Uncle Miles said nothing, but as though pulled by a magnet we walked slowly up towards the stage. The stillness was odd, after the clamour of children's voices. Elaine put her hand on my arm and shivered.

"He's gone."

I shook my head. "He has nowhere left to go."

As we neared the front of the stage the back curtain parted and Monsieur Magique appeared again. He had taken off his pierrot's dress and bobbled hat and most of the greasepaint, and he was recognisable. Elaine cried out. "Ulfheim." And then, with that instinct for self-justification I had come to recognise, she added: "I told you he came from France."

"You were perfectly right."

The man on the stage made a mocking bow to us all, and vanished again behind the curtain. Uncle Miles called out something unintelligible. Betty and I stepped up on to the stage, and as we did so heard the sound of the shot.

Behind the curtain there was a tiny dressing-room, with a few improvised shelves, some boxes of tricks, clothes on hangers, a cracked looking-glass in front of a battered dressing-table. He lay on the floor with the revolver beside his hand still smoking, and a hole in his head as neat as that in Blakeney's.

"The end of Ulfheim," I said. "The dead who won't awaken."

Betty stood with her hands in her trouser pockets, looking down at him. Uncle Miles had turned away, a handkerchief to his eyes. His shoulders were shaking.

"It was clever of you to guess," Elaine said. "I don't see now how you did it."

"He left clues. Not so much clues as jokes, really. Like Stiver and Strawman and Ulfheim. In the play Ulfheim is a landowner."

"Oh. But how did you know it was David?"

"Not David," I said. "Hugh."

Chapter Sixteen

Treasure Island

"A special sense of humour," I said. "The Wainwright sense of humour you might call it. Hugh was devoted to Ibsen. When he was looking for a new name to give Blakeney, Stiver seemed to him a good joke, and it must have seemed a better one still, when he was talking to us at Folkestone to use the name of a character in a play called *When We Dead Awaken*. He couldn't resist making the whole thing a kind of puzzle to which we could guess the answer if we understood the rules. In that way he must have been rather like you," I said to Miles.

It was the afternoon. The four of us were sitting—at last —in the Deux Magots drinking coffee, after a long session with the police and a visit to Hugh's room in the rue Peter Paul where we saw his few possessions. It had been decided by Uncle Miles, for once assuming the burden of responsibility, that Hugh should be buried in Paris, and Miles had decided also that he would wait until we returned to Belting to tell the rest of the family the truth. Betty now said in response to my last words, "He was nothing like as nice."

"So Ibsen struck one chord in my memory, if you like to

call it that. And then last night when Fallon talked about the magician, going back to the magician, it struck another chord. I remembered how Monsieur Magique had had a booth on the beach at Folkestone and that he'd left it unexpectedly, and I understood too what it was that I had seen when Ulfheim opened his case in the restaurant that day. The wires and figures were those of puppets. So I knew this morning that we were looking for Monsieur Magique, and that he would be Hugh."

"You've been very clever," Elaine looked distastefully at a bearded man who was drinking Russian tea from a saucer.

"What I still don't understand in my addled way is this," Betty said, bobbing her bronze head. "What was the reason for this whole elaborate fandango? Why wasn't Hugh's family told he was still alive, and why didn't he come back when the war was over?"

"That's easy." I looked at Elaine. "It wasn't David who killed your uncle. It was Hugh. Arbuthnot hinted that to me, but I didn't understand him. You must have known he was suspected, Uncle Miles."

"You must remember I was away at the time, and when I came back Hugh and David had both been killed. That is, we thought they had. Mamma didn't encourage anything being said about that other regrettable affair."

I sipped my coffee, which was black and sweet. "The way it worked out must have been something like this. Hugh and Sullivan were partners in this firm of estate agents. You remember, Elaine, how surprised your father was that no money was left when the firm was wound up, that the winding-up was in the hands of Lady W—Lady Wainwright—and that she was quite generous about it and that your father got his money back. I think there was a good reason for that. Hugh had been cheating Sullivan. Sullivan found out, they had a row outside the pub that night and Hugh killed him. Isn't it right—about Hugh cheating Sullivan, I mean?" I asked Miles. "Stephen must have known."

He coughed unhappily. "Mamma did mention something about it, although not in those words. She said money was missing and that she had made it up. After that she didn't refer to it."

"I'm sure she didn't. Now, before Sullivan's body was found, Hugh had gone overseas and had been reported missing, believed dead. In the meantime the police must have discovered that Hugh had been robbing Sullivan, perhaps they even had a witness who saw them together that night. But though they may have been satisfied that Hugh was the murderer, what could they do about it? Hugh was dead, killed in action. The natural thing was to let the case drop. They must have satisfied themselves that David had nothing to do with it. In the report of the trial I read it was the coroner who asked David awkward questions, not the police. Now do you see why Hugh couldn't come back? He would have been arrested for Sullivan's murder."

I paused and asked for more coffee. When it came I continued. I really felt like a detective.

"I don't suppose we shall ever know what happened to Hugh in 1944. He must have known that his position was desperate, that at any time he might be ordered back to England to be questioned about Sullivan. The official story was that he had got separated from his platoon and was never seen afterwards. My guess would be that he managed to surrender to the Germans, and then worked for them. In fact it's more than a guess, if you remember that snap." The snap was among Hugh's meagre effects. It showed him wearing the uniform of the Free British unit that the Germans had tried to organise, a cap stuck on the back of his head, his arms round the shoulders of two SS officers. "When the war was over he must have managed to slip back to France like a lot of others, and there assumed the name of Roger Lorraine." It was under this name that Hugh had been living in the rue Peter Paul. "I dare say he had half a dozen other names before that."

Uncle Miles sighed. "It's a most distasteful story. I must telephone Mamma to let her know that we are coming back. I suppose one can telephone from this place."

"Wait a minute." I raised a finger, combining the role of detective with that of the Ancient Mariner. "There isn't much more. We don't know what Hugh did for a living, except that the police told us he became Monsieur Magique three years ago, and that he'd got no criminal record. The idea of substitution must have occurred to him when he met Blakeney, and learned that Blakeney was a survivor from the plane in which David had been killed. He knew his mother had adored David, he knew she was likely to accept anybody who came back and produced reasonable credentials. Of course the deception couldn't be maintained indefinitely, and he must have told Blakeney that it wouldn't have to last long. Once the will had been changed, Blakeney could say that he just wasn't able to settle down again at Belting. He would go off, assisted if he was lucky by an allowance from his mother. When she died he would return to claim the money and then go off again, splitting the money with Hugh. All he had to do was to pass muster for a week or two and with the intensive training Hugh gave him, plus his own knowledge of David, that shouldn't be impossible. It was a wild scheme perhaps but the stakes were high, and after all what had they got to lose? Markle was hired to give Blakeney a bit of moral support, and in case he ran into real trouble he could refer to Hugh, who had managed to get an engagement in Folkestone as Monsieur Magique.

"The scheme came unstuck, we know, but not because of Blakeney. He couldn't have lasted out much longer probably, but he played his part well. The trouble came because Hugh was reckless enough to stay in Filehurst, where Thorne recognised him. He killed Thorne, but of course that brought the police down on Belting, and once they'd started to investigate, Blakeney was certain to be exposed. Hugh came back to Paris and Blakeney followed him. He must have threatened Hugh with exposure, so Hugh killed him too. But he knew the game was up, really." I said the thing that had been in my mind ever since I saw the body in the little room at the back of the marquee, the mouth still set in its mocking smile. "I wish I'd known him. He must have been an interesting man."

Miles looked at me, sighed again, and went away to telephone.

Elaine said, "I think he was horrible."

"Christopher's a romantic," Betty remarked, rather as she might have said that I was an Albanian. We looked out at Paris flowing past us. On my left, inside the café, two Americans were arguing about existentialism. My stomach was quiescent. I was proud of my detective skill. Life seemed very good. I hardly looked up when a voice said hallo. It was Norman Beaver. He spoke to Betty. "I've been looking for you all over, Bets. There's a Yugoslav painter I want you to meet—"

Betty shook her bead. "Nix on Yugoslavs. I'm going back to England."

"You are? What for?"

"I'm getting married."

"Who to?"

"My ex. We settled it last night."

"You did?" Norman did not seem surprised, but his interest in Betty noticeably diminished.

"It's time I settled down."

"I expect so. And the best of luck to you both."

He was gone. I said congratulations. Betty looked at me with a considering eye. "Why don't you two get married?"

Elaine and I began to laugh together, as we had laughed last night. Elaine said, "I was waiting for him to reach the age of consent."

"I was meaning to ask you," I said, "but I've been too busy."

Somehow a bottle of champagne appeared. I goggled at Betty. "Don't tell me you own this place too."

"As a matter of fact I don't, this seemed to be a toast-drinking occasion, that's all. But perhaps you'd prefer that snake juice—"

"No, thanks."

We had almost finished the bottle when Uncle Miles reappeared, his face preternaturally solemn. "Yours is flat, but you'll have to drink it just the same," Betty said.

Uncle Miles took his glass, absent-mindedly gulped it down, then addressed me. "Christopher, Mamma is dead."

• • ● • •

It began to rain when we returned to England, and it was still raining when we buried her in Filehurst churchyard.

A dozen people stood by the graveside as the coffin was lowered into the earth. She had died on the morning that we had found Hugh, and I was glad that she had never learned the truth about Hugh and David, but had died in the belief that her son had come home. With this feeling there was another too, one which I did not like to acknowledge, relief that her benevolent tyranny was over and that my own independent life was about to begin.

Humphries, bowler hatted and wearing a black tie, was waiting for us when we got back to the house. He read the will in the drawing-room. Stephen was itching to ask questions, but Humphries shook his head. "I think it will be best if I read the will first, Mr Wainwright." Stephen began to tell him about David, but the solicitor interrupted. "With your permission, Mr Wainwright, I should prefer to read the will."

He sat in an arm-chair, took stiff sheets of paper out of a long envelope, and began. "This is the last will and testament of me, Jessica Mary Wainwright…" How easily I could summon up the image of her on that first afternoon in Woking, with her hair piled up under the tall hat with the feather in it, and how long ago that seemed. But what was Humphries saying?

> "… I give to my three children, David who has recently returned to me, Stephen and Miles, an equal share in all my goods and property. I wish to express my appreciation to Stephen and Miles, and to Stephen's wife Clarissa, for the devotion with which they have looked after me in my declining years, and I should like to say how sure I am that their care for me has not been motivated by any thought of future gain. If it were otherwise I would be grievously disappointed, and so would they.
>
> "To Christopher Barrington I leave the sum of two hundred and fifty pounds, with my thanks for his help with the book about the Egyptian Wars. I

trust that he will one day complete this, and that it will bring him a considerable financial reward.

"To Ellen Peterson I leave the sum of one hundred pounds, with thanks to her for the years of faithful service she has given…"

Two hundred and fifty pounds. I could hardly take it in. I looked at Stephen and Miles and saw that they were as bewildered as I. Humphries finished reading, coughed, and began to fold up the will. Stephen broke silence, speaking in a kind of high-pitched gasp. "I don't understand. What does it mean?"

"It means, Mr Wainwright, that your mother had very little money to leave. She made the few bequests you have heard, and divided the rest equally among her children. There is the house, of course, but it is mortgaged."

"Mortgaged! But Mamma was *rich*."

"I am afraid not. She was left sufficiently well off when her husband died, but perhaps she was never quite as rich as you may have thought."

"I thought there was—would be—two hundred thousand pounds." Stephen stopped, as though conscious of the impropriety of naming a sum.

"Oh dear me no, there was never anything like that, nor even half of it. And then during the five years after the end of the war she plunged quite disastrously in the stock market. Strongly against my advice, I need hardly say. Recently she has speculated less, but even so her income had been further reduced. In a few years' time things might have become very difficult indeed."

"Do you mean there is *nothing*?" Stephen could not control the shrillness of his voice.

"There is a certain amount in the bank, and there are a few shares that are worth something. And there is the estate. It is mortgaged, as I mentioned, but for considerably less than its value. Lady Wainwright realised, however, that it would be impossible for any of you to maintain it. It will have to be sold."

Uncle Miles began to laugh, not hysterically but with genuine amusement. I had never liked him so much as at that moment. "It's like *Treasure Island*, isn't it? You remember when they found Flint's treasure chest, and it was empty. It was all for nothing, our staying with Mamma all these years, and Hugh's trick was all for nothing too. Dear Mamma, she's certainly had more brains than her sons."

Clarissa bayed deeply. "It's an outrage. After all the years we spent looking after her. An outrage."

"I shall want to see the figures." That was Stephen again. His voice had come down a note or two.

"By all means," Humphries said coolly. "Whenever you wish."

"I dare say there'll be a few thousand for each of us," Miles said cheerfully. He turned to me. "But what about you."

"Two hundred and fifty won't see me through the university."

"It certainly won't. What will you do?"

"I shall get married."

Epilogue

All this happened a long time ago, and it seems even longer than it is. Elaine and I didn't share a wedding with Uncle Miles and Betty as they suggested, because I hadn't got a job. In the spring of the following year, however, I became a reporter on a Sussex paper, and we decided not to wait any longer. A couple of years later I moved to a national, the *Banner*, and a year after that our son was born. We gave him Hugh Blakeney as Christian names. Our daughter, born a couple of years later, was named Betty, and Betty Wainwright is her godmother. Soon after that I was made Washington correspondent of the *Banner*, and I've been there ever since. I like the life. Elaine gave up working before Hugh Blakeney was born, and never went back to it.

I come to England four weeks in every year, but find it rather slow and smug. Elaine often comes with me but one year when she didn't, and when I'd been down to Sussex for lunch with an aspiring politician, I took a wrong road back to London and was surprised to find myself within a few miles of Belting. It seemed natural to turn the car's bonnet that way.

I nearly passed the drive, because it had been so much changed. There were concrete gates and a sign that said:

Experimental Weapons School, Admin. Branch (E). There was a man in uniform on the gate, but a good many trees had been cut down and I was able to see the house. It looked smaller than I had remembered, and it no longer reminded me of a church but seemed to be simply a piece of ugly red Victorian Gothic. I stared at it for a few seconds without feeling anything, and then drove on.

I have never seen Stephen since I left Belting, but I believe that he and Clarissa are now breeding dogs in Dorset. We exchanged Christmas cards for a year or two and then dropped it. Miles is still married to Betty, and I believe they are very happy. We see them rarely, but Miles still writes me chatty letters, which I answer with shorter and less interesting ones. Betty insisted that he must have a job, and bought an advertising business for him, which Miles runs. I have his last letter in front of me now.

> The routine is fairly boring, but I *do* like writing copy. Here is my latest masterpiece, written for Bronk's steak and kidney pies. Mum is leaning out of the window calling to the children, a Bronk's pie piping hot on the table behind her. She calls:
>
> *Jack and Jill and George and Sidney,*
> *Come and get it! Steak and kidney!!*
> *Growing girls and boys all just*
> *Adore its crispy flaky crust.*
>
> Good, eh? Anyway the client liked it.

Most of my youthful notions have been forgotten, and I doubt if Betty would call me a romantic now—even *abroad* is not what it was since I've been living there so long—but when I read one of Miles' letters the past comes up vividly.

I see again the arrival of the claimant in the courtyard on that July day and am taken back to the world of Belting, to the strippling ream and the daylight lamps in the corridors and the battle of Tel-el-Kebir laid out on the floor of the Pam Moor.